PRAISE FOR ANNIE REED

"One of the best writers I've come across in years. Annie excels at whatever genre of fiction she chooses to write."

— KRISTINE KATHRYN RUSCH,
AWARD-WINNING WRITER/EDITOR

"You can't go wrong with Annie Reed. Her deftly-crafted tales—with characters as memorable as the stories themselves—far surpass most of what's out there. She deserves a wide audience."

— MICHAEL J. TOTTEN, AUTHOR

"Annie's writing is magic, seriously."

— ROBERT J. MCCARTER, AUTHOR

"Annie Reed is considered by many to be one of the best new writers appearing in fiction."

— DEAN WESLEY SMITH, EDITOR
PULPHOUSE FICTION MAGAZINE

A CHRISTMAS REUNION

ANNIE REED

TV Ink
Thunder Valley

INTRODUCTION

This book began life as a short story called "The Reunion."

I loved how that story turned out, but when I finished it, I discovered that I wanted to know more about the two characters at the heart of the romance. I wanted to meet their children and their friends. And most of all, I really wanted to see how they spent Christmas Day.

Initially I thought the answers to all those questions would result in a novella, but it seemed they all had much more to say. I love it when something like that happens because it means that characters came alive, which is a wonderful thing for writers and readers alike.

I hope this full-length version of Jeannie and Raymond's Christmas love story will be as fun to read as it was for me to write.

CHAPTER 1

$\mathcal{D}$ecember. What an odd time for a high school reunion.

Especially a twenty-*fourth* high school reunion. Didn't those things happen in multiples of five after the tenth or so?

Jeannie Carlson settled down with her morning coffee and her tablet computer in what had become her favorite spot ever since she'd come to stay with her daughter—an overstuffed barrel chair in the sunroom in her daughter's little house. The glass-walled, climate controlled little space, with just enough room for the chair and a little wicker loveseat and a small glass-topped occasional table, was a perfect place to soak up the sun without actually having to brave the Arizona heat.

She loved living with her daughter. The house was a cozy two-bedroom with an upscale kitchen, a small living room, and the sunroom right off the dining room. Kristen had furnished it with a mishmash of styles, from the wicker loveseat in the sunroom to a floral print living room sofa straight out of the '80s, but it all seemed to work somehow. The home had become a refuge for Jeannie at the time when she needed it the most. In fact, the only thing she didn't like about living with Kristen was the climate.

She really should be used to Arizona weather by now, but except for the horrible, humid summer months when she and her husband had lived in Sacramento, nothing had prepared Jeannie for the never-ending sunbaked heat of Arizona. She'd been living with her daughter for nearly nine months now, but she still wasn't acclimated.

November in Arizona didn't feel like autumn. She hadn't thought even once about breaking out one of the lightweight cotton sweaters she'd worn in Sacramento during the last few months of the year. And forget about the comfortable bulky sweaters she used to wear when she still lived in the Pacific Northwest. Those were still packed away in storage.

"Iced coffee, Mom," her daughter Kristen always told her whenever they discussed Arizona's hot, dry climate. "The secret is to start your day with iced coffee. Or an iced latte."

At least she hadn't suggested iced tea.

Jeannie had always preferred coffee to tea, and she liked her coffee hot. Especially in the morning. She'd gotten in the habit during her senior year in high school when the bell for her first class rang at seven-thirty. While her best friend Marta Gilroy usually got a latte or a large soda whenever they stopped at the convenience store on their way to school, Jeannie had always gone straight for the coffee.

Nowadays she could afford a far better quality of coffee than the bitter old convenience store stuff, but she still wanted her coffee hot. She readily admitted that where coffee was concerned, she was stuck in her ways. But it was a small thing, and so many things had changed over the last year, she supposed it was only natural to insist that this one small thing stay the same.

She leaned back against the comfortable cushions in her chair and opened her tablet to reread the email she'd received that morning from Marta.

After high school graduation, she and Marta had gone their separate ways. Marta had gotten a scholarship to a prestigious art school in New York. She'd fallen in love with life on the east coast and decided to make New York City her home, and gradually she and Jeannie had lost touch.

Jeannie had stayed in their hometown, a little town outside of Portland, Oregon, mainly because she'd fallen in love and married a remarkable man right after high school. Jake had been a mature man of twenty-five to Jeannie's eighteen, and he'd been the love of her life. She'd gone to a local community college to learn business and took design classes through a local company at night. After she'd graduated, the company had offered her a permanent position.

They'd lived in the same hometown for over fifteen years, then Jake's company had transferred him to California, first to Monterey and then to Sacramento. With

Jake's help and the blessing of her former employer, Jeannie had started her own graphic design business, working with most of her clients over the internet so that she could continue her career no matter where Jake's company sent him.

Jeannie had liked Monterey. Living so close to the ocean, that part of California had reminded her of Oregon. But the company only kept Jake in Monterey for six months before transferring him to Sacramento.

Neither of them had liked Sacramento at all. After years of living in the Pacific Northwest and then on the California coast, being stuck smack dab in the middle of the state felt like living on another planet. They made frequent trips to San Francisco just to spend time by the ocean whenever Jake's schedule allowed, and one glorious week they traveled to Seattle so that Jake could attend a conference.

By that time their daughter was going to college in Arizona—a truly foreign land (all that desert!)—and they'd begun to think of life after Jake retired and collected his pension. Both of them had decided life in Oregon had suited them best, and they'd started to plan for an eventual return home.

Then Jake had suffered a sudden, massive heart attack in January, one week shy of his fiftieth birthday. He'd passed away in the ambulance, and Jeannie had become a widow at forty-two.

Marta had sent Jeannie a heartfelt condolence card along with her phone number and a photograph of herself in front of a gallery showing of her art. Marta still looked like the Marta of Jeannie's memories. Marta had been goth in high school before goth was a fashion statement, and in the picture she was still dressed in black. A long, flowing black skirt, a silky black poet's blouse, and metallic blue extensions in her straight black hair.

The picture had made Jeannie's heart ache. She'd called Marta, and after a few awkward moments, Jeannie had felt the years melt away. Marta was still the same brash, in-your-face person she'd always been. Marta had listened while Jeannie told her about her life with Jake. She'd been a strong shoulder when Jeannie cried and had even made her laugh over shared memories.

They'd ended the call with a promise to stay in touch this time, and they had. Mostly through emails with the occasional marathon phone call.

Kristen had suggested that the two of them try Zoom, but Marta had balked.

"Too much like scheduling a business meeting, and that's all kinds of wrong," she'd said.

That was fine with Jeannie. Zoom and Facetime were perfectly good tools, but they didn't appeal to her. Not even in her business. It was one of the little quirks Jake used to tease her about. He said it made her adorable. She thought it made her old-fashioned, but she still preferred an email or a phone call any day of the week.

She'd called Marta the week before to wish her a happy birthday instead of sending a card. Marta, an early November baby, had responded in typical Scorpio fashion.

"Forty-two and perpetually single," she'd said. "Don't remind me."

Not that Marta really seemed to mind. She'd never married because, as she said, she'd never found a man she wanted to spend more time with than in her studio painting—so long as there was a well-muscled model in the vicinity.

Jeannie was single now too. That fact still stung—not as much as it used to, but the hurt was still there. She knew that wasn't what Marta had intended by her remark, it was just Marta being her blunt and brash self. If anything, living for a couple of decades in New York City had made Marta even more Marta than she'd been in high school.

They'd laughed and chatted. Marta had talked about a new gallery showing scheduled for the beginning of December. Jeannie had told her about a new client who wanted the same basic graphic designs as his hottest competitor—only better.

"That's why I don't work for other people," Marta had said. "People in general are nuts. You were always better at dealing with people than I ever was."

Jeannie didn't know about that. She'd been a wall-flower in high school. She didn't have to deal with people because no one really noticed her. Marta, on the other hand... With her black clothes, black hair, black finger-nails, and an in-your-face attitude, she wasn't someone people could ignore.

"You could make it in the art world, you know,"

Marta had said. "With original works. You say the word, and I'll introduce you to the right people."

Jeannie had demurred—politely but firmly. Art was what had initially brought the two of them together, but they'd gone in totally different directions since graduation.

They met thanks to several art classes they'd shared in high school—back when most high schools still offered classes like that. Marta had worked with all sorts of mediums, from charcoal to clay, producing evocative and memorable works. Some of her negative space charcoals had been downright breathtaking.

While Marta had created moody landscapes and stunning figure work, Jeannie had preferred sketching buildings, bridges, still-life arrangements, or basically anything with sharp edges that she could soften with watercolor paints, which became her favorite medium. Then one of her art teachers had introduced her to computer graphics.

Jeannie had loved the freedom that computer graphic programs gave her. She discovered that she could play around with different styles, brushes, patterns, and colors, and if something didn't work right, she could just delete it. Working on paper or canvas had always made her concentrate on her mistakes instead of just enjoying the creative process.

No wonder she'd gone into the computer graphics business. Her company, a one-woman operation, did well enough for itself that she was considering whether she needed to bring on a support person to do all the administrative tasks so she could concentrate on the design side of the business. It would have to be someone who could work remotely like she did. The last thing she wanted was to open an actual office. She was too used to working in the little sunroom in Kristen's house so she wouldn't have to venture into the Arizona heat.

Every now and then she thought about playing around with watercolors, but she hadn't gone past the thinking-about stage. If she let Marta talk her into displaying original artwork, not only would she have to push past the little self-critic who lived in her brain and only saw the flaws in the things she painted on paper, she'd have to travel to a gallery and attend meetings in person to pitch her art to someone who'd no doubt criticize her efforts as well. None of that sounded appealing.

Jake had nudged her a time or two in that direction, but those had been gentle nudges. Everything about Jake had been gentle and kind.

Jeannie shook her head. Her thoughts had certainly gone off on a tangent, hadn't they?

After their last phone call, she hadn't expected to hear from Marta again right away, especially since she'd be knee deep in preparing for her December gallery show. This morning's email had caught Jeannie by surprise. So had the attachment—an invitation to their Twenty-Fourth High School Reunion.

To be held two weeks before Christmas.

Can you believe these people? Marta had written. *Life in the suburbs must have eaten their brains.*

Jeannie had been living in the suburbs, more or less,

ever since she'd been married. Even now Kristen's house was a nice little two bedroom in a neighborhood of nice little one- and two-bedroom houses in what passed for the suburbs in Arizona. But she was pretty sure Marta didn't mean to bunch her in with all the rest of their former classmates whose brains had been eaten away by their suburban lifestyles.

Who schedules a high school reunion in the middle of December anyway? Marta's email went on. *And what kind of notice is this? A month, at this time of year?*

According to the invitation, the Twenty-Fourth Reunion of Everett Parker High School's graduating class of Nineteen Ninety-Eight would be held the second weekend in December. There would be three separate events—a charity golf tournament in the morning on Saturday (weather permitting), a dance at the high school gym on Saturday night, and a champagne brunch on Sunday. The reunion committee asked the recipient, in this case Marta, to forward the invitation to any classmates who might have moved out of the area.

I have no idea how they got my email, Marta had written. *I'm sending this along in case they don't have yours.*

The committee apparently didn't since Jeannie hadn't received an individual invitation. She wasn't surprised. She'd changed her name when she'd married Jake—she'd been Jeannie Bishop in high school—and with all the moves they'd made since she'd graduated, she probably wasn't all that easy to find.

Marta, on the other hand, was still Marta Gilroy. Jeannie imagined everyone remembered the loud, brash, goth girl, and she'd had several well-publicized showings of her art.

Jeannie took a sip of her coffee and scanned the names of the people on the reunion committee. She only recognized one of the women—Cissy Hollenbach, former head cheerleader. Definitely not someone Jeannie had been friends with in high school. The names of the other members of the committee didn't ring a bell, although she'd probably seen them in the hallway between classes, or she might have even had them in one of her classes. High school had been a long time ago.

Twenty-four years, to be exact.

Let me know if you plan to go, Marta had written in her email. *I'm not sure I can swing it, with the gallery thing and all, but I wouldn't mind checking out the old place. But not if you're not going because what fun would that be?*

Oh crap. I've written a double negative, haven't I? Mrs. Trotter would be scandalized.

Jeannie chuckled. Mrs. Trotter, their shared English teacher, had been fifty if she'd been a day, oh so terribly old to the teenagers they'd been. She wore reading glasses on a pink beaded chain around her neck, and her thick gray hair hung halfway down her back. She was a stickler for grammar, and Marta—to put it mildly—wasn't.

Mrs. Trotter was no doubt long retired, if she was even still alive.

Jeannie looked out the window at the bright Arizona sunshine. Instead of shrubs and planters thick with flowering plants, Kristen's postage-stamp backyard was edged with several varieties of cactus and succulents.

She wouldn't mind seeing her old hometown again. She missed green. She missed rainy, overcast days. She even missed the damp air that made her short dark hair frizz. Kristen loved the desert and planned to stay in the southwest, if not in this little leased house—her starter home, as she called it. Jeannie knew she wouldn't be able to live with her daughter forever—the arrangement had never been intended to be permanent, after all—but she'd been dragging her heels trying to decide what to do.

Would going to the reunion be the right thing to do? She'd had some good times in high school, but in retrospect they all seemed to involve Marta and art. If her old art teacher was there, the one who'd introduced Jeannie to computer graphics, she could buy the woman a long overdue drink as a way to thank her for pointing Jeannie in the right direction, career wise.

But what if Marta wasn't there? If Jake was still alive, Jeannie would be happy to take him, show him a bit of her past before they'd met. And show him off a little too. But Jake wasn't alive, and if she went, she'd be going alone.

She sighed and closed the email. She moved it to the folder where she saved all her personal correspondence. She'd respond to Marta later, but right now, it was time to get to work. She had a new design she was working on, something that actually appealed to her: a new logo for a self-help center that worked with at-risk teenage girls. She was doing the work at half her normal rate, donating the rest of her time, and the design was coming along nicely.

High school was such a long time ago. She had her life and she had work she enjoyed. She had a daughter she loved and who loved her. The last thing she needed was to go to a high school reunion and see all her happily married former classmates.

This Christmas was going to be difficult enough— her first Christmas without Jake. She didn't need the reminder from strangers that she was all alone.

CHAPTER 2

Raymond stared at his computer, not quite believing what he'd just read.

The morning had started out well enough. His first cup of coffee tasted great. The view from his office window gave him a great view of downtown Portland, Oregon, and for once that view wasn't obstructed by fog or rain. His receptionist, a petite young woman with a tendency to overshare the details of her personal life, had even arrived at work early and given him a sunny smile.

She'd gone out on a date the night before, and apparently it had gone well. Raymond wasn't about to ask because he didn't want the gory details. His real estate firm was more like one big happy family than a high-pressure business—two of his agents had been with him since they'd gotten their licenses—but still, even families kept some things to themselves.

At least no one in his work family was still trying to

set *him* up on a date. Pretty much the last thing he wanted to do right now was date.

A perfect example of why was the email he'd just received from his ex-wife Belinda.

We're going to have to rearrange Thanksgiving, she'd written in her terse, take-charge style. *Todd's giving a presentation at a conference in Seattle on Monday, so we're renting a place on Bainbridge for the long weekend.*

Of course, they were.

Belinda's new husband came from old money, as she was fond of working into almost every conversation, and apparently he still had a lot of it. Todd could certainly afford a short-term rental on Bainbridge. The island just outside of Seattle boasted some of the most expensive real estate in the area, and that was saying something. The place they were renting probably looked like a castle.

That wasn't the part that hit him in the gut, though.

We're leaving on Wednesday, the email continued. *Todd told Marri about a holiday street festival on Bremerton on Friday. We're going to take the ferry over from Bainbridge so she can see Santa.*

I'm hoping you won't make a fuss about this.

Make a fuss? No, of course not. Why would he? Just because he'd been planning to spend the whole Thanksgiving weekend with his daughter. (Their daughter, he corrected.) Was looking forward to it in the way a man who loves his child with his whole heart does when he can't spend nearly enough time with her.

Raymond and Belinda had been married nearly a decade before Marrissa came along. They'd all but given up on having any children when Belinda discovered she was pregnant.

Belinda had always been an independent woman. She'd had a career of her own as an interior designer, which had seemed to mesh well with Raymond's career in real estate. Right up until Marri was born.

Nearly two years to the day after that joyous event, Raymond had gone to his lawyer's office to sign off on a joint custody agreement in conjunction with the divorce proceedings Belinda had filed.

A year after that, the judge who'd signed their divorce decree issued an order allowing Belinda to relocate out of the state to Tacoma, Washington—where her new husband Todd lived and worked—and to take Marri with her. The order had relegated Raymond to a non-custodial parent with liberal visitation rights. Marri had only been three years old at the time. The day Belinda and Marri left for Tacoma had broken Raymond's heart.

In the three years since, he'd spent a good deal of time commuting between Tacoma and Portland so that he could spend time with his daughter. If he only had a weekend, he'd rent a house so that he didn't have to waste any precious time with his daughter commuting back to Portland. But when they had an entire week together, he took her back to his house in Portland so they could spend that week doing the kind of things a dad with a young toddler could do.

Like watch kids' shows on television, make popcorn in an air popper, play with her favorite toys, and sing off-key along with a karaoke machine his staff had given him as a joke a few years before Marri had been born. Marri loved to sing all the songs on the tv shows they watched, and he'd started to teach her songs he enjoyed. This year he was planning to teach her some new Christmas songs he remembered from his childhood.

One thing hadn't changed when Belinda had moved to Tacoma with Marri, and that was their holiday schedule with Marri. According to their custody agreement, Raymond and Belinda were supposed to alternate Thanksgiving and Christmas so that the years he had Marri for the Thanksgiving weekend, she'd be with Belinda and Todd on Christmas Eve and Christmas Day. On the years he had Marri for Christmas, she spent Thanksgiving with her mother and stepdad.

This was supposed to be Raymond's year to have Marri for the Thanksgiving weekend—next weekend— and Belinda knew that. She'd still decided that Marri should spend Thanksgiving with her and her husband, and had given Raymond less than a week's notice.

And without consulting him ahead of time. Of course.

And she'd done it in her usual devious manner—by pitting his daughter against him but not in an obvious way.

Raymond pinched the bridge of his nose against an impending tension headache.

His daughter—*their* daughter, their daughter he had to remind himself again—was only six years old. Santa Claus was still a big deal in her life. One of the songs he'd planned to teach her was "Santa Claus is Coming to

Town." If Todd had told her about going to see Santa at the festival on Bremerton, as Belinda had told Raymond, she'd already be brimming with excitement.

He could push the matter. Threaten to take Belinda to court for violating the terms of their custody agreement. But Thanksgiving was next weekend, and he knew without even calling his lawyer that he'd never get an order requiring Belinda to comply with their custody agreement in such a short period of time. If anything, she'd get a slap on the wrist from the judge along with a stern *Don't ever do this again or you'll face sanctions*, which wouldn't change anything.

And even if he could get an order and Belinda decided to comply with the order, did he really want to break his daughter's heart like that? In her mind, she'd always associate him with missing Santa Claus. Thanksgiving wasn't a big deal to a six-year-old, not with Christmas right around the corner.

He was the grownup here. He had to think of what was best for his daughter, and in this instance, that meant keeping his anger and disappointment in check and be the bigger man.

His heart could take it, right?

Right.

He hit *reply* on his laptop, then stared at the blank message window.

He knew what he *wanted* to say. He wanted to tell her that he'd already made plans to pick Marri up next Wednesday—that he'd bought nonrefundable airline tickets months ago (which he had)—and he'd be happy to drive Marri back to Tacoma on Friday morning, even though he was supposed to have her for the whole weekend. Tacoma wasn't that far from Seattle—or Bremerton, for that matter. Belinda and Todd could make the trip on Friday, no sweat, and still take Marri to see Santa before catching the ferry to their rented castle on Bainbridge Island.

It was a compromise. A reasonable comprise. Which was why he knew Belinda would never go for it.

Somewhere along the way, probably during those first ten childless years of their marriage, Belinda had become a very selfish woman. He would swear on his deathbed that she hadn't been that way when he'd married her. She'd been loving then, if a little self-centered, but still loving.

Then she'd changed. Maybe it had been the demands a new baby made on her, but she'd started to complain about the hours he put in at work. About how her own work was falling behind. He'd suggested that they hire a nanny—they could certainly afford it—but she'd flat out refused. Then he'd offered to hire household help. She'd refused that, too.

"Marriage is supposed to be a partnership," she'd argued. "*You're* supposed to be the one helping me."

So he'd rearranged his work schedule so he could be home more often. He'd helped around the house, only then she complained that he got in the way.

He came to understand that no matter what he did, it would never be enough.

Somewhere along the way, she'd stopped loving him.

She loved their daughter, he never doubted that, but she didn't love *him* even though he loved both of them with his whole heart. He'd still loved her when he'd signed the divorce papers.

It had taken him a long time to get over her. Now she was just his daughter's mother. Unfortunately, she was also someone he had to continually deal with even when he didn't want to.

Raymond took another sip of his cooling coffee as he considered whether he should wait to reply to give himself time to get over his initial anger and disappointment. One thing he'd learned in business was to always take a moment before responding to something that either annoyed or insulted him or his clients, like a ridiculously lowball offer on one of the properties he had on the market. He should probably do the same thing in this case.

He certainly had enough things to keep him busy. He was planning to spend the day at an open house that started at eleven. With downtown traffic, he needed to leave shortly in order to give himself time to pick up some fresh flowers on the way. He'd convinced the owners to add a small occasional table to the entryway to put fresh flowers on—a trick he'd actually picked up from Belinda years ago. Fresh flowers, she'd said, made a place look loved and cared for.

The property was in a difficult neighborhood, and while the house itself was in remarkably good shape, it was still going to be a tough sell. The sellers were motivated—they were scheduled to relocate to southern California after the first of the year in connection with the husband's employment—and Raymond hoped to snag some interested buyers with today's open house.

He sighed, shut his eyes briefly, and took a couple of deep breaths. The difference between the anger he felt at Belinda's email and the annoyance he felt at a lowball offer on a property was that this time it was personal. This was about his daughter. *His* daughter. In his head he knew he needed to put Marri first, which meant giving in to Belinda. He just needed to convince his heart, and the only way to do that was to get it over with. Otherwise, he'd be thinking all day about what he should say instead of giving his entire attention to the open house.

His mother always told him to get the hard stuff out of the way, and then the rest of the day would be a breeze.

He put his hands on the keyboard and started to type.

I bet Marri's excited to see Santa. Don't let her ask for a pony. I've already said no.

He stared at the last two sentences. It was true, more or less. One of the shows they watched was *My Little Ponies.* The last time they'd watched it, Marri had said she wanted a pony of her own.

He'd patiently explained that real ponies didn't have the same powers as the ponies in the cartoon. That they could be messy and smelly and could be mean. (He'd heard somewhere, probably from someone at the office, about a pony that had bit a child at a petting zoo.) Marri had said that *her* pony would never be mean, but by the end of their weekend, she'd forgotten about the whole thing.

If he put a bug in Belinda's ear about a pony, that would practically guarantee she'd talk Todd into buying one for Marri for Christmas.

He sighed. He hit the backspace key until he'd erased the sentences about a pony. He didn't really want to be *that* guy. The one who put his daughter in the middle of a war between her two families. It wasn't her fault her parents had gotten divorced.

Still, he needed to at least mention Christmas. If he didn't, Belinda would just assume he'd conceded both holidays to her this year.

After you get back, he typed, *we can finalize when I'll be picking Marri up for Christmas.* Then he added *Have a nice Thanksgiving.*

He usually signed his first name above the professional signature his program always inserted at the end of his emails. This time he didn't. He just sent the reply.

Switching holidays was only fair, but she hadn't treated him fairly in years. She'd probably come up with a good reason to keep Marri over Christmas too.

But that was a battle for another day. A battle he hoped he wouldn't have to wage. Today he had an open house that would hopefully end in a few reasonable offers.

The brochures he'd prepared for the open house were already in his briefcase. With the flowers he still had to pick up, the brochures, and the smell of a fresh pot of coffee he'd make every hour or so, he hoped to give the property a nice homey feeling.

That was one thing he missed living on his own. His house was just a house. It became a home when Marri was with him.

It was amazing how much one little girl had changed him, and changed him for the better. He still worked hard at his business, but business wasn't his entire life. Maybe the divorce had been a wakeup call. A reminder that he was more than just a realtor. He was a dad.

He straightened his tie and picked up his briefcase and tried—unsuccessfully—not to think about how much he was going to miss his daughter. He could find something else to do over Thanksgiving weekend. There was always work. He could make a few calls, follow up on a few leads.

But hadn't he just told himself business shouldn't be his entire life? Even when he didn't have Marri?

Well, there were always football games to watch on turkey day. He'd played football in high school and still caught a game every now and then. He supposed he could donate the turkey in his freezer to a homeless shelter and get a burger at his favorite restaurant downtown.

The one thing he wasn't going to do was ask any of the single women he knew—not that he knew that many —out on a date. Eventually he might like to spend time with a woman again. He might even consider getting married at some point in the future.

The far future.

Of course, he'd have to meet the right woman.

And with the way he felt about women right now, thanks to his ex, he was pretty sure that wasn't about to happen.

Ever.

CHAPTER 3

The aroma of fire-roasted green chilis and fresh cilantro filled Kristen's house with the promise of a spicy, delicious, and healthy meal.

Kristen had come home from work with a bagful of ingredients for a southwestern dish that was high on vegetables and light on meat. Jeannie was actually surprised at the small package of chicken breasts. Most of the meals her daughter prepared were strictly plant based.

Since she'd moved to Arizona, Kristen had adopted a mostly vegetarian diet. She'd also started jogging a few days a week as a way to cope with the stress of college and work.

Casual jogging had turned into a passion for running. Now Kristen ran in various charity events when her school and work schedules allowed. She was currently training for a marathon she'd be running in January.

Jeannie had never been as dedicated to exercising as her daughter. She and Jake used to take long walks in the neighborhood in the evenings, both as a way to work out the kinks after sitting at computer desks all day and to spend some extra time together, just the two of them without work interrupting them. Jeannie still walked in the evenings sometimes, especially when Kristen had night classes and wasn't home until late, but more often than not she'd just curl up with a good book.

The change in her diet and the walking had done wonders for Jeannie's figure. She hadn't gotten on a scale, but her clothes fit better than they had in years. She'd even bought herself a few new outfits that were two sizes smaller than what she usually wore. She'd thought of herself as pleasingly plump ever since her first year in high school when she'd inevitably compared herself to some of the other girls in her class, especially the super-slim cheerleaders.

Marta had also been pleasingly plump, although Jeannie'd never told her that.

Well, Jeannie certainly wasn't pleasingly plump now. Her waist was actually slim. So were her hips. And she had collarbones. Who knew? She certainly felt healthier than she had in years.

It helped that Kristen was a fantastic cook. The food she prepared tasted better than most restaurants, although there were times when Jeannie still missed a nice medium-rare steak.

Kristen gave her a sideways look as she chopped onions at a butcher-block cutting board. "I need to talk to you about something," she said, "and I don't want you to take it the wrong way."

Jeannie paused stirring the mixture of corn, chilis, tomatoes, and garlic simmering in a spicy sauce on the stove. In her experience, a lead-in like that never boded well.

"Is everything all right?" she asked.

Kristen had a lot of things going on in her life. She was in graduate school and working fulltime in an accounting firm. She was also dating a nice man she'd met at the firm over a year ago. Michael was only a couple of years older than Kristen and handsome in an understated way. The dating had turned serious during the last several months. He'd even started calling Jeannie "Mom." She wouldn't be surprised if he gave her daughter a ring this year for Christmas.

"With me?" Kristen said. "Everything's fine. It's you I'm worried about."

What?

"I'm fine, too," Jeannie said. She backed away from the stove to let Kristen dump the chopped onions into the saucepan. "You don't need to worry about me."

At least not anymore.

Jeannie could admit to herself that she'd been a wreck after Jake had died so suddenly. They'd been living in Sacramento for a few years, but all of her friends had been *their* friends, or more precisely, Jake's friends through his work. Jeannie hadn't made any close friends of her own, mostly because she didn't like the city and hadn't planned to stay after Jake retired. After he died, his friends had drifted away.

Kristen had flown to Sacramento to help Jeannie

with the arrangements for his funeral, but she couldn't stay as long as either of them had wanted. After she flew back to Arizona, Jeannie had turned into something of a hermit.

She'd always thought of herself as a competent woman. Independent. Able to make her own decisions, but all of a sudden every choice she had to make was hers and hers alone. She was no longer part of an "us." She no longer had anyone to bounce ideas off of. To come to a consensus about, or if their opinions differed drastically —which was rare—to come to a compromise. Things as simple as what to eat for dinner suddenly seemed impossible to make.

She hadn't been able to keep that from her daughter.

"You're grieving, Mom," Kristen had told her. "Everyone experiences grief differently. Things will get better. They won't be the same, but they'll be better."

Kristen had been right. How she'd gotten so wise, Jeannie didn't know. Maybe she'd learned about emotional responses to loss in one of her college classes.

The biggest decision had been the most impossible to contemplate. Jeannie didn't want keep living in Sacramento. Jake's employment had kept them there, but Jeannie could live anywhere with a stable internet connection and still do her work. She certainly didn't want to keep living in the house she'd shared with Jake. It had been too big and too empty without him, and she'd grown to hate it. But she just couldn't make a decision about where she wanted to live.

Kristen had solved that problem—at least

temporarily—by inviting Jeannie to come live with her. "I don't like the idea of you being all by yourself right now," she'd said. "Sell the house or keep it and rent it out until you decide what to do with it, but I'd like you to come live with me. At least for a little while."

At least the decision about what to do with the house had been an easy one. She'd put the house on the market. It had sold quickly, and a month later Jeannie was sharing her daughter's house. Jeannie paid half the expenses, which she told herself gave her daughter a little financial breathing room, if a little less actual room since even with two bedrooms, Kristen's house wasn't all that large.

"I know you're fine," Kristen said as she chopped more tomatoes and onions for a homemade salsa for the organic tortilla chips that went with dinner. "But I think you're hiding out here, and I don't think that's good for you."

Hiding out?

Okay, yes, there were some days that Jeannie didn't leave the house. And yes, she hadn't made any friends here. When she went for walks in the neighborhood in the evenings, she'd wave a friendly hello to any neighbors who were out and about, but she never stopped to actually talk with any of them.

"Have you given any thought to going to the reunion?" Kristen asked.

"Not really," Jeannie said, although that wasn't quite true.

She'd told Kristen about the email from Marta and

the invitation to the reunion. Kristen had chuckled at the idea of a high school reunion two weeks before Christmas. "What were they thinking?" she'd said, unintentionally echoing Marta's sentiments.

But neither of them had mentioned the reunion since. They'd been too busy making plans for Thanksgiving. Kristen's boyfriend Michael was going home to Minnesota to visit his parents for Thanksgiving this year so they wouldn't be too disappointed when he spent Christmas in Arizona with Kristen.

That meant it would be just Jeannie and Kristen for Thanksgiving dinner. It had gone without saying that Kristen wouldn't be cooking a turkey and neither one of them wanted to try a vegetarian turkey substitute. Jeannie had insisted on stuffing—some traditions just shouldn't be broken—although they'd be stuffing a pumpkin. That alone should make the meal interesting.

It had also gone without saying that both of them would miss Jake. Kristen hadn't had Thanksgiving dinner with her parents for years, but Thanksgiving dinners at home had always been the three of them. Jeannie hoped that the odd menu would make the day seem less like Thanksgiving and more like just any other Thursday, only a Thursday when Kristen didn't have school or work.

Still, the reunion had been at the back of Jeannie's mind. She'd found herself thinking about her high school days at odd moments. Wondering what the old high school looked like. What some of her old classmates looked like. Even wondering what her old hometown looked like these days.

"Is Marta going?" Kristen asked. "Has she decided?"

Jeannie shook her head. "She hasn't said, but it doesn't look good." Marta wasn't exactly a starving artist, but Jeannie got the idea that her old high school best friend couldn't afford a round-trip airline ticket from New York to Portland at this time of the year.

"And you don't want to go by yourself." Kristen dumped the tomatoes and onions in a mixing bowl and added chilis, spices, and chopped cilantro. "I understand that. It's like the terror of going to a prom without a date."

Jeannie had only been to one of her own proms. Not by herself, and it had ended badly. She'd never talked to her daughter about that. Kristen had gone to each of her proms, and she'd always gone with a date and come home beaming.

Kristen gave Jeannie another sideways glance. "You know, you could poke around town while you're there. Maybe look at a few houses? Check out the listings."

Jeannie started to protest, but Kristen just grinned at her.

"This is going to sound horrible, especially since I invited you," she said, "but you can't keep living with me." She held up a hand to keep Jeannie from protesting. "I'd keep you here forever, it's not that. I just know you're not a desert person, and this is about as desert as you can get without moving to someplace like Palm Desert or Death Valley."

Jeannie sighed. "You're right," she said. "I'm just not sure where..."

She trailed off. Even after all these months she had no idea where she wanted to live. She knew where she *didn't* want to live. Sacramento was high on that list. So would be... what had Kristen said? Palm Desert? Death Valley? Both of them sounded horrible. All she knew was she wanted to live somewhere that was green at least part of the year.

"So use the reunion as an excuse to check out the area," Kristen said. "Cruise around the old hometown. See if any of your favorite haunts are still there."

"Haunts?" That sounded quaintly old-fashioned.

"You know what I mean." Kristen bent to get a bowl out of a low cabinet for the tortilla chips. "I wonder if that old 7-Eleven is still there. Or the Dairy Queen on the corner by Beth's house."

Oregon used to be thick with Dairy Queens, especially on Highway 101 along the central coast. Dairy Queen had been high on the list of hangouts for Kristen and her friends, especially her best friend Beth. Jeannie hadn't been to a Dairy Queen in more years than she could remember. She didn't even know if the franchise was still in business.

"And while you're at," Kristen said, "you can think about whether you'd like to move back. The way you and Dad planned..."

This time Kristen trailed off. Jake's sudden death had been hard on her. He'd been so young. Jeannie was sure

Kristen had expected to have her dad around for years to come.

Jeannie put an arm around Kristen's waist and gave her a hug. "I'd be leaving you alone right before Christmas. I was hoping we could do a few of the things we used to do as a family for the holidays."

"Like trim a tree?"

"That would be nice," Jeannie said. "If you even have Christmas trees here. That aren't cactuses."

Kristen arched an eyebrow in mock annoyance. "We have Christmas trees here," she said. "Artificial. I have a small one in a box in the garage. And a few ornaments."

Most of the Christmas decorations Jeannie had were in storage, including ornaments Kristen had made in grade school. Kristen had taken a few with her when she'd moved to Arizona to go to college. Those were probably among the ornaments she had in her garage.

"We can put up the tree before you go to the reunion," Kristen said. "That's the good thing about artificial trees. You can leave them up forever and they're not a fire hazard."

One other holiday tradition from Kristen's childhood was probably out. "No cookie baking though, I'm guessing," Jeannie said.

Kristen shrugged. "I'm sure I can dig up a couple of recipes that'll work. No fruitcake, though."

Jeannie wrinkled her nose and let go of her daughter's waist. "Those were horrible," she said.

One of their neighbors in Oregon, back when Kristen had been a pre-teen, used to give everyone on the block a homemade fruitcake. She was a sweet woman who'd never married. She'd inherited the house she lived in from an elderly relative, and apparently had inherited the fruitcake recipe as well. Jeannie always ate one slice just to be polite, but after taking one bite, Kristen and Jake had flat out refused to eat any more.

"But we can still make cookies together," Kristen said. "I'd actually kind of like that."

Making cookies, just the two of them, had been a family tradition from when Kristen could barely reach the countertop in their old house. The kitchen had been thoroughly dusted with flour by the time they were done, and the cookies didn't always resemble the pictures in Jeannie's recipe books, but they tasted delicious.

"Does Michael like cookies?" Jeannie said. "We can always make an extra batch when I get back so we make sure to have enough for Christmas day."

"You know, I'm not really sure," Kristen said. "He's never eaten any around me, but he could just being doing that to be polite since I don't eat a lot of sugar."

They went on like that while they finished preparing dinner. Talking about old family traditions, like singing Christmas carols on Christmas Eve with the only light in the house coming from the twinkle lights on the tree, and having hot chocolate with mini marshmallows on Christmas morning before they opened any presents. And somewhere between dishing up the two chicken breasts Kristen had cooked in that marvelous southwestern sauce and dipping her first tortilla chip into her daughter's delicious homemade salsa Jeannie realized that she'd made a decision about the reunion without even realizing it.

She'd be going. To her Twenty-Fourth high school reunion, even though she'd never been to any other reunion and even though she'd be going by herself.

This was either a brilliant way to spend some time in her old hometown while she surreptitiously looked at possibly moving back, or it was the worst idea in the history of bad ideas.

She wouldn't know which one until she got there.

Two weeks before Christmas.

Ho, ho, ho.

CHAPTER 4

Raymond had made a terrible mistake. He'd agreed to meet his cousin for coffee at a trendy new café but, of course, Lucas had an ulterior motive.

"Will you be my plus-one for the reunion? *Please?*" Lucas looked at Raymond with those puppy-dog brown eyes of his that he'd used to such great effect back when they'd still been kids.

Those eyes had gotten Lucas into—and out of—more trouble than a man had any right to get into. Especially a forty-two-year-old gay man who had his own successful clothing line and who, with his three business partners, owned three separate malls in the Portland area.

Raymond had brokered the deals on two of them.

They were sitting at a two-top near the rear of the café. The place had a Middle Earth theme, with movie memorabilia and artwork decorating the walls, along with photographs—some of them autographed—of the actors featured in the various Rings movies. The two-top was directly opposite the wall featuring an autographed picture of Legolas.

Lucas had chosen the table. He'd had a huge crush on Orlando Bloom when the first movie came out all those years ago. Apparently his crush hadn't completely gone away.

"Can't you get a date for the reunion?" Raymond asked.

He wasn't really in the mood to go anywhere. Last weekend had been depressing, even though Belinda had let Marri call him on Friday to tell him all about her visit with Santa. The call had been brief, like all calls with his six-year-old daughter. And while he'd enjoyed hearing her voice and especially hearing the excitement in her voice, the call had only served to hammer home how much he missed her.

He'd still been subdued when he'd gone back to work yesterday. Mondays were usually madhouses, everyone busy with the behind-the-scenes work involved in marketing and closing sales on all sorts of properties. He'd managed to wrangle a decent deal for the owners of the difficult property—the open house, and especially the flowers and free coffee—had worked. After a series of offers and counteroffers, the sale was finally going through. The owners were ecstatic, the buyers excited, and Raymond?

He couldn't work up a bit of enthusiasm. He'd even handed off the paperwork to one of his assistants, which he rarely did.

When Lucas had invited him out for coffee, his assistant had practically pushed Raymond out the door.

"Go," she'd said. "This is Tuesday. Nothing urgent happens on a Tuesday, and you need some cheering up."

He wrapped his hands around his mug. He'd ordered a holiday blend called Gimli's Grog, which turned out to be just the right combination of rich dark espresso roast with a hint of cinnamon and dark chocolate. The day had dawned cold and cloudy, and a misty rain had been falling for the last hour. The stoneware mug was warm enough to take the chill off his hands. Any other day and he might have ordered one of the scones on the menu, but today all he felt like was coffee.

Lucas had ordered a skinny latte named Elven De-Lite. With his purple-framed reading glasses and shiny purple raincoat, he would have been the most flamboyant elf in Middle Earth.

"Are you crazy? I'm not taking a *date* to my high school reunion," Lucas said. "I'd never hear the end of it. That's nearly as bad as taking a date to a wedding."

Lucas's mother—Raymond's aunt—was forever after the both of them to settle down. She thought she'd finally gotten through to Raymond after he'd married Belinda, but at least she'd left him alone after the divorce. No hints about getting back in the saddle. Lucas, on the other hand, now got the brunt of his mother's need to play matchmaker. Unfortunately for his mother, Lucas didn't have the temperament to stay with just one Mr. Right and raise a bunch of kids.

"Why are you even going?" Raymond asked. "You

were miserable in high school."

Raymond was a couple of years older than Lucas, and they'd gone to different high schools. Raymond had achieved some modest popularity, thanks to being on the football team. He'd never been as popular as the quarterback or the star receiver, but he hadn't been subjected to any of the bullying that always went on in every school he'd ever attended. He stood up for the kids he'd known who were being bullied, but he hadn't been able to do anything for Lucas.

Raymond thought Lucas had been one of the bravest kids he'd ever known. He'd come out in middle school, which made him the brunt of every gay joke known to teenagers, which was bad enough. But a few times Lucas had come home with scrapes and bruises that he hadn't gotten in P.E. His mother would call Raymond's mother, and Raymond would end up hearing all about it.

"There was only one person you even liked all that much," Raymond said, "if I'm remembering right."

Lucas had made one good friend in high school, an art student who'd been an outcast in her own way. Raymond had seen her on occasion at Lucas's house, and she'd seemed like a nice person.

Lucas put his latte down on the table and looked at Raymond over the top of his reading glasses. "Are you seriously asking me why I'm going?" He held his hands out wide, the better to show off his shiny purple raincoat, no doubt one of his company's designs. "If you were as rich and successful and utterly fabulous as I am, wouldn't you want to rub it in all their snooty faces?"

Raymond had to admit that Lucas had a point, but he felt like he should point out the obvious. "You know you'd be perpetuating a stereotype," he said.

Lucas chuckled. "All the better to mess with their heads." He gave Raymond a wicked grin. "At least I'm not asking you to go in drag."

"Good God, no."

Raymond loved his cousin, but there were limits.

He glanced over at the autographed picture of Legolas. He'd never read *The Hobbit* or *The Lord of the Rings*, but he'd enjoyed the movies well enough. Belinda hadn't liked any of them. She hadn't even liked going to the movies all that much. Raymond had gone to a movie by himself on Thanksgiving after none of the football games had held his interest. He couldn't even remember now what movie he'd seen.

One thing that had stuck with him about the *Rings* movies though, even after all these years, was the loyalty of that blond-haired elf to his friend Aragorn, the reluctant king. Legolas had gone into battle at Aragorn's side again and again even though the odds were overwhelmingly against them.

Raymond hadn't been able to stand up for Lucas when they'd been in high school. He could either be a jerk now and tell Lucas no, or he could be a good friend and just agree to go to the reunion. It wouldn't be as bad as facing an army of Orcs commanded by an evil wizard. It would just be a bunch of middle-aged people trying to relive their glory days. What was one evening out of his life anyway? It wasn't like he had any better offers.

He sighed, and then he gave Lucas a rueful smile. "I'm not dancing with you," he said.

"I wouldn't expect you to," Lucas said in all seriousness.

"And we're not holding hands."

One corner of Lucas's mouth quirked up. "That's fine," he said.

"And no kissing!"

Raymond felt that had to be said right up front. Lucas was heavily into playacting when he was "on," and Raymond wouldn't put it past Lucas to plant a big sloppy kiss on Raymond's mouth just to make a point.

Lucas's mouth fell open in mock surprise and he pressed a hand to his chest. "Oh, no! Be still my heart!"

Raymond snorted, feeling a little silly now that he'd even brought that up.

Lucas's expression turned serious. "So does this mean you'll go?" he asked. "You're not just teasing me?" He glanced down at his hands. His nails were immaculately manicured, as always. "I just don't want them to think I'm a sad, lonely gay man."

Puppy-dog eyes were one thing, but this was raw, honest emotion. How in the world could Raymond say no to that?

"Okay," he said. "I'll go."

Only later did he realize that he should have set one more condition, especially with a gay man who owned his own clothing line.

He should have told Lucas that he'd only go if he could wear his own clothes.

CHAPTER 5

Jeannie slid her carry-on beneath the seat in front of her, tucked her paperback book into the seatback pocket, and sat down in her window seat.

Whenever she'd flown with Jake, she never needed to bring a book. They'd always chatted away during the entire flight, or they'd doze off leaning against each other. This time she'd brought two books. The second one was inside her carry-on just in case she couldn't lose herself enough in the first one to forget how nervous she was.

She still couldn't quite believe she was on her way to the reunion. Or more precisely, to her old hometown. She hadn't made up her mind whether or not she'd actually go to the dance tomorrow night. Maybe just the Sunday morning brunch. That would be safe enough, wouldn't it?

She'd gone to plenty of lunches by herself when Jake was still alive. But going to the dance by herself—that might be too much like going dateless to a prom. Especially since the one prom she'd gone to had been held in the same school gymnasium where the reunion's dance was being held on Saturday night. Going dateless to a dance was the mark of a high school loser, according to all the popular girls who'd never seemed to lack for a date.

Jeannie settled back into her seat and clicked the seatbelt around her newly trim hips. She didn't feel smaller, especially not two sizes smaller, even though the slacks she'd bought to wear to the dance—*if* she decided to go—were definitely two sizes smaller. The clerk at the clothing store Kristen had taken her to last weekend had told Jeannie she could probably wear a size smaller yet, but Jeannie wasn't ready to wear something that form fitting.

She glanced out the window at the brilliant, cloudless Arizona morning. The last time she'd been on a plane had been when she went with Jake to Seattle for his conference. The day had been overcast then with a heavy smog layer in Sacramento thanks to late season wildfires burning in the south. Even though it had been overcast and chilly in Seattle, the smoke-free air had been a relief.

She'd had the window seat on that flight too. Jake had sat in the middle seat so that she could watch the plane take off, leaving the ground far behind.

The flight from Sacramento to Seattle had been relatively short, and they'd spent the time talking about what things they wanted to do after he retired.

Jake wanted to travel, and not just the kind of trips

they could take during his vacations from work. He wanted to Travel, he'd said, with a capital T. So to pass the time they'd made a list of places to go and things to do.

Jeannie still had that list in a note on her cell phone.

He'd said he wanted to go to Paris so he could walk along the Seine and see the Eifel Tower in person. Jeannie had never been to Washington, D.C., and she told him she might like to go just to see all the monuments. She'd also said she might like to go to Hawaii one day.

He'd told her those were fine places to visit, but they weren't Travel with a capital T. If she was going to dream about what they'd do one day, she should dream big.

How big, she'd asked.

He'd grinned at her and said New Zealand.

Of course. She should have known. He wanted to go to New Zealand to see where the *Lord of the Rings* movies had been filmed.

"Maybe even bungee jump off that bridge," he'd said. "You know the one."

They'd watched the special features on one of the DVDs of the movies—Jeannie couldn't remember now which one—and one of the actors had talked about how he'd bungee jumped off a bridge somewhere during filming. Jeannie didn't think Jake really wanted to bungee jump. He just wanted to see where it had happened. He'd said there was a tour now of the area where they'd filmed the scenes in the Shire, and that was something he'd like to do one day.

He'd always dreamed big, even if his reality was quite a bit tamer.

He only had two vacations a year. They spent one visiting Kristen after she'd moved to Arizona, and they always drove so they could take their time getting there. On the way, they'd stop overnight in Las Vegas. They'd dress up and go out to a romantic dinner and then they'd take in a show. On the way back home, they'd stop in Reno for one last quiet night before getting back to the real world, as Jake used to call it.

He always took his second week of vacation around the holidays. That was usually a staycation, as Kristen called it, with maybe a day trip to San Francisco or drive along the coast to the redwoods, weather permitting. Otherwise, they stayed home, decorated their house for Christmas, watched holiday movies, and stayed up far too late on Christmas Eve. "Waiting for Santa," as Jake put it.

They both knew it was a holdover from when Kristen had been little. Parents of small children always stayed up late on Christmas Eve playing Santa for the kids. In Kristen's case, that meant putting a few toys together—like the two-wheel bicycle Santa left for her one year—and last-minute gift wrapping.

And taking a conspicuous bite out of the cookies Kristen had set aside for Santa.

Jeannie had threatened to leave milk and cookies for Santa at Kristen's house this year. Kristen had retorted that at her house, Santa got health food energy bars and drank unsweetened almond milk, and liked it.

A silver-haired woman stopped at Jeannie's row, interrupting her reminiscences.

The woman peered at the boarding pass she held in one hand. "I believe I've got the aisle seat," she said with a smile. "With any luck, we won't have anyone in the middle."

Jeannie smiled back. "That would be nice," she said.

Another plus for driving instead of flying: no crowded airplane seats. Jeannie had never been uncomfortable when she and Jake drove somewhere on their vacations, although when Jake sat in the middle seat, he was the only one who got crowded.

She'd thought briefly about driving to the reunion instead of flying. She'd have to stop somewhere overnight, but she'd driven from Sacramento to Arizona when she'd moved in with Kristen. Driving to Portland would take just one more day.

The problem was the weather. "There are just too many mountain passes," Kristen had said when Jeannie'd first talked about driving. "At this time of year, they can be pretty dangerous."

Neither one had said "for a woman alone," but they both knew that was what Kristen had meant. Jeannie had never changed a flat tire, and although Jake had shown her how to put tire chains on their car, she'd never done it herself. When it had been the two of them driving somewhere, she'd never worried about the weather.

The woman settled into her aisle seat. She was a generation older than Jeannie. Her silver hair was cut shorter than Jeannie's, and she wore it in a tightly curled style that accentuated her delicate features. She had a paperback book as well, but she held hers in her hands.

The lights on the plane flickered and a thump vibrated the floor beneath Jeannie's feet, and the plane began backing away from the terminal. Jeannie took a deep breath to steady nerves that had jumped up a notch.

She was really doing this. Going back to her home-town, a place she hadn't visited since Jake's company had transferred him to California. What would that be like? They'd lived together there for over fifteen years after they got married. Her favorite places had become their favorite places. She'd be seeing him everywhere she went, and that would make her miss him all the more.

She hadn't considered that part when she'd decided to fly back to the place she still considered home.

"Nervous flyer, dear?" the woman asked.

Jeannie tried not to look startled. Were her nerves really that obvious?

Or maybe it was the way she was gripping the armrest. She was holding it so tightly her knuckles had turned white.

"I never used to be," Jeannie said. She made herself relax her hand. "It's been a long time since I've been on an airplane." And then she hadn't been alone.

"Just take a few deep breaths," the woman said. "And when the attendant comes to ask if you'd like anything to drink, see if they have one of those little bottles of brandy and dump some in your coffee."

She said that last with a definite twinkle in her faded

brown eyes. She must have been a hoot when she'd been younger.

"I'll keep that in mind," Jeannie said. Not the brandy in her coffee—it was still too early in the morning for that—but taking a few deep breaths might help.

The plane began to roll forward to take its place in the line of jets waiting for a runway. Jeannie turned her attention back to the window. Up front, one of the flight attendants was giving the in-flight safety speech. She was a pretty girl, just about Kristen's age, and she was wearing a Santa hat at a jaunty angle.

Jeannie only half listened until she realized that the normal safety speech had been replaced with a version that was a riff on the old "Night Before Christmas" poem. She turned her attention back to the front of the plane and listened—really *listened*—to the poem. And she wasn't the only one. Even the passengers who'd struck her as jaded frequent flyers were all watching as the attendant injected a little Christmas spirit into probably the most mundane part of her job.

When the attendant finished, most of the passengers gave her a hearty round of applause, including the silver-haired woman in the aisle seat.

"Now, wasn't that fun?" the woman said to Jeannie. "And would you look at that." She glanced at the middle seat, which remained empty. "A little unexpected holiday floor show and a bit of room to spread out. Wherever you're going, I'd say we're both off to a good start."

Jeannie didn't believe in omens, and her faith in good luck had taken a major blow when Jake died before he got to travel to any of the places he'd dreamed about. But she still hoped this woman was right.

Maybe good things were about to happen. Or at least one more good thing. Her own mother had believed that good things came in threes, and Jeannie had just experienced two.

The plane took its spot on the runway. Jeannie leaned back in her seat, ready for the push against her back as the plane built up enough speed for takeoff.

Was she due for one more piece of good luck? Something beyond her luggage arriving at the same time she did?

She took another deep breath and let it out slowly.

She certainly hoped so. Christmas was supposed to be the season of miracles, after all. She was ready for one more good thing.

She just had to get the reunion out of the way first.

CHAPTER 6

Raymond's assistant gave him a decidedly odd look as she carried a hanging suit bag into his office. Instead of stately black, the bag was brilliant purple and emblazoned with the logo of Lucas's clothing company.

"Were you expecting a delivery?" she asked.

In point of fact, he was expecting closing documents to be delivered on the house for the couple who were relocating to California. As difficult as the property had been to sell, once the offers and counteroffers had finished flying back and forth and the final contract had been signed, the actual sale had gone relatively smoothly. He was supposed to receive the final documents today, and the sellers were standing by to review and approve the documents as soon as the messenger delivered them to Raymond's office.

But as usual for a Friday, especially a Friday in December, things were taking their sweet time. Even in these days of email and electronic signatures, some things still had to be handled on paper with honest-to-goodness signatures, and real estate transactions were one of them.

He hadn't, however, been expecting anything from Lucas.

The reunion dance at Lucas's old high school was tomorrow night. Raymond had planned on wearing casual slacks and a conservative sports coat. As a nod to the season, he'd dug out an old holiday tie his staff had given him one year at the firm's annual Christmas party. He'd never worn the thing, and figured this would be as good a time as any.

Knowing Lucas, almost anything could be inside that suit bag.

He took the bag from his assistant and hung it on the garment hook on the back of his office door.

"I'm not sure I want to open this," he said.

She gave him the raised-eyebrow look she used whenever he asked her to do something he knew would be impossible for anyone else in his office to accomplish in the amount of time it needed to be done.

"Will it explode?" she asked.

Not likely. At least not in the traditional sense, but the shiny purple raincoat Lucas had worn to the coffee shop was one of his more subdued designs.

Raymond was about to ask his assistant to leave so he could discover whatever was inside the bag in privacy, but gossip that was high on speculation and low on facts about the actual contents of the bag would burn through the office faster than a wildfire. Besides, it might be an early Christmas gift. Lucas had given him gifts in the past, including a surprisingly traditional tuxedo, complete with a cashmere scarf, when the deal on the second mall Raymond had brokered for Lucas and his partners had closed.

Of course, chances were slim this was anything normal, given that the reunion dance was the following night. Especially since Lucas had admitted he wanted to show off his fabulous self.

Just please don't let it be a dress. Raymond had specified that he wouldn't go to the dance in drag. He'd make an ugly woman. He just didn't have the facial features for it.

He unzipped the bag and opened it gingerly.

It might as well have exploded.

The shiniest, *greenest* suit Raymond had ever seen in his life hung inside.

"Oh, *my…*" his assistant said.

He'd been so startled by the suit, he'd actually forgotten she was still there. Her eyes were wide, and she had one hand over her mouth. Probably to stifle a smile. Her eyes certainly held a great deal of amusement.

At least she wasn't laughing.

"I'm going to kill him," Raymond muttered.

Now she did chuckle, something she squelched when he shot her a glare.

"Are you going to a costume party?" she asked.

He hadn't thought so. "A reunion," he said. "With Lucas."

His assistant had worked for him for the last eight

years. She knew most of his immediate family, including Lucas. She also knew about his clothing line (she'd been more than impressed with the tux), but Raymond doubted she knew the depths that Lucas would go to when he wanted to prove to the snobby people he'd gone to high school with that he was a fabulously successful, truly *fabulous* gay man.

To be fair, Raymond hadn't thought Lucas would go this far either.

"You agreed to go to a reunion?" she asked. "With Lucas? Are you crazy?"

He sighed. "Temporarily insane. He asked me right after Thanksgiving."

"Oh," she said, her smile fading.

She knew how horrible Thanksgiving had been for him. She also knew how his ex had come up with excuse after excuse for why he couldn't have Marri for a weekend since Thanksgiving. Belinda was probably still annoyed that he'd pushed her about swapping holidays so that he could have Marri over Christmas, especially since she knew Raymond was right. She'd eventually agreed that he could pick Marri up on Christmas Eve—in the afternoon, she'd pointedly said—and keep her until the following Monday.

While he was looking forward to having his daughter on Christmas morning—there was nothing like watching his daughter come running down the stairs, her eyes wide at the realization that Santa had actually come and left her presents while she slept—by the time Christmas rolled around, it would be more than a month since he'd seen her the last time, and that was far too long.

"At least it's a nice shade of green," his assistant said. "Not, like, neon green or anything."

That was true. Although the suit was shiny—probably some type of silk instead of wool—and looked like something a Hollywood star might wear to a movie premiere, the color was somewhere between Christmas tree green and a nice, ripe avocado. On the inside.

His assistant tilted her head as she stared at the suit. "More like a bell pepper."

Great. He was going to the reunion dressed like a salad bar.

He moved the jacket to one side just to check, and sure enough, the suit pants were the same color. A pocket square of rich burgundy matched the color of a shirt on a separate hanger. Next to the pocket square was a silk tie of a slightly different shade of green shot through with horizontal gold stripes.

He also knew without looking at the sizes that the suit would fit him perfectly. Lucas had made the tux for him, after all, and Raymond still wore the same sizes now as he had then.

"At least he didn't send me green shoes," he said, then he shot a look at his assistant. "He didn't send another box along, did he?"

She shook her head. "No, no shoes. Basic black should work, I think."

Good. Something to look forward to—wearing his

own shoes. He didn't need to go to a reunion in a high school gym wearing very new, very slick dress shoes.

He stood back and glared at the suit. He was wrong. He wouldn't be going to the reunion dressed as a salad bar. He was going to look like the world's largest North Pole elf dressed up for a night on the town.

He shooed his assistant out of his office and closed the door. Then he called his cousin.

"Did you get the delivery?" Lucas asked before Raymond even said hello. "What do you think? Isn't it fabulous?"

"Yes," Raymond said. "Fabulous. Except you forgot that I'm not."

"Oh, posh."

Raymond could almost see the dismissive expression on Lucas's face.

"Everyone is as fabulous as they want to be," Lucas said. "You just have to let your inner gay man out to play."

"I don't have an inner gay man. Or an outer gay man." Raymond pinched the bridge of his nose against an impending headache. "I'm a boring heterosexual man who likes his boring business casual clothes."

Lucas didn't have a snappy comeback. In fact, he went quiet.

"Puppy dog eyes won't work," Raymond said. "We're not on a Zoom call."

Raymond didn't particularly like video teleconferences, but they were a necessity in his field. He purposefully hadn't call Lucas on Zoom because he *didn't* want to see his cousin's patented pout.

After another pause, Lucas said, "You really don't like it? I gave you the most conservative of the two."

"This would only be conservative if I was walking the red carpet next to someone dressed in shiny black vinyl and carrying a whip," Raymond said.

Then he realized the rest of what Lucas had said.

"What do you mean, 'of the two'?" Raymond asked.

Lucas sighed. "They're a mirror image set," he said. "Part of my *Apparel of Many Colors* line. You have the green suit. I have the burgundy suit. I introduced these colors for Christmas this year. They're really very popular."

He sounded upbeat there at the end.

Raymond felt like a heel. This wasn't just Lucas being over-the-top fabulous. This was advertising for his clothing line. This was business, and Lucas had always supported Raymond in his.

Okay, so Raymond would be embarrassed like crazy to walk into the gym wearing a suit like the green bell pepper monstrosity, but he'd agreed to go to the reunion for his cousin, after all. Lucas was successful by anyone's standards—except maybe his own—and showing off his company's products was part of showing off exactly how successful he'd become.

Lucas was going to the reunion to be noticed. To be appreciated, and maybe to be liked for who he really was by the people who'd ignored him in high school. Or who'd made his life a living hell. The mirror image suits would certainly get the both of them noticed.

Raymond told himself again that it was only one evening out of his life. He could either stay home by his miserable self, missing his daughter, or he could make his cousin happy. He'd have to wear the suit, but it would probably look terrific on him (except for the color). Lucas worked with some incredible designers and tailors. The tux had fit Raymond better than any suit he'd ever owned. Certainly better than the tux he'd rented for his wedding to Belinda.

"Okay," he finally said. "I'll wear the suit. But we're not going to dance together."

They'd probably look like cellophane-wrapped Christmas packages on a dance floor.

"But we're going in together," Lucas said. "I want to make an entrance."

Of course he did.

"No holding hands, remember?" Raymond said.

"I'm guessing that means no hand in the crook of an elbow either."

"Absolutely not," Raymond said.

He had a sudden feeling that he was negotiating a deal, with offers and counteroffers flying back and forth, just like when he was representing clients in a real estate transaction.

He had one more condition to add to his counteroffer.

"We walk side by side," he said. "And no posing for 'couples' pictures, or snapshots together in a photo booth." He didn't know if the reunion would have one, but considering he'd been blindsided by the suit, it was probably a good idea to cover that contingency as well.

"Agreed," Lucas said, a little too quickly. "Anything else?"

Raymond thought about what other things Lucas might have in mind. Nothing came to mind.

"Can't think of anything," he said.

"Good," Lucas said. "I'll have limo pick you up at six tomorrow night. See you then!" And he disconnected the call.

A limo?

Raymond sighed.

He hadn't thought of that, and maybe he should have. Limos and prom nights went hand in hand, but reunions? It wasn't like he was Lucas's date.

So what else hadn't he thought of? The possibilities were mindboggling.

This one night out of his life might be a very, very long night after all.

CHAPTER 7

*J*eannie stood by herself at a bar that had been set up at the far end of the gym. She was waiting patiently for one of the bartenders—*Jimmy Jones, Chess Club President,* his nametag read—to mix her rum and Diet Coke, light on the rum.

A part of her still couldn't believe she was back in her old high school. Before she'd gone into the gym, she'd wandered down the halls, just taking it all in. The floor was still the same faded gray linoleum and the lockers still the same industrial gray, but the walls had been repainted a subtle shade of dusty blue that made the halls seem light and airy. She couldn't remember her locker combination from her senior year, but she did find her old locker. A top locker, thank goodness considering all the heavy books she'd had that year. The second locker to the left of the art room.

The art room had been her favorite place, the classroom where she'd felt most at home and most accepted. Did the art students now feel the same way? She hoped so.

Kristen hadn't shared Jeannie's love for art, but she'd inherited some artistic ability. The way she'd decorated her house told Jeannie that her daughter had an artistic eye for detail and what shapes and colors went together, even if Kristen didn't consciously realize it.

Jeannie had tried the handle to the art room but the door was locked. She'd peeked in through the small square window in the door. She didn't know what she was looking for exactly, maybe just another connection to her past, but the room was dark. All she could see were a few easels on the near side of the room.

It might be a cliché, but the easels looked so small. The whole school looked smaller than it had when she'd gone here. She'd passed a few other people out wandering the halls like she was, and she's caught snatches of conversations. How small the school felt to everyone seemed to be a common topic.

She'd expected that when she'd gone to parent-teacher conferences when Kristen was still in elementary school, where the student desks were so tiny. But high school should have been different. By time she'd been a senior, she was only a year away from getting married, although she didn't know it at the time. She'd felt like an adult with adult-sized desks and chairs and adult-sized easels in art class.

You're putting this off, she'd told herself. Just go to the gym already. Get it over with. She'd feel better once she could blend in with the crowd. After all, who—really—was going to notice her?

Of course, she hadn't counted on having to walk through an arched trellis covered in red, green, and white balloons. The trellis had been set up right on the other side of the gym doors. As if that wasn't bad enough, a spotlight illuminated the other end of the trellis. A spotlight! So much for making a quick, anonymous entrance.

She'd walked through that tunnel as quickly as she could without looking like she was actually running. Kind of the way she'd eaten Brussel sprouts when she'd been a kid—do it fast and get it over with.

She'd breathed a sigh of relief when no one announced her name, like she was a contestant on a game show or a celebrity arriving at a red carpet premiere. She was just Jeannie Carlson—Jeannie Bishop when she'd gone to school at Parker High—and no one's idea of a famous celebrity. Marta could have pulled off an entrance like that, but Marta wasn't here.

Once Jeannie had speed-walked through the trellis and zipped through the spotlight, she'd paused to get her bearings. The last time she'd been in the gym had been the final assembly of her senior year. The one where awards had been given out for things like perfect attendance and perfect citizenship. The stage band had performed, and so had the school's spirit squad—with Cissy Hollenbach, head cheerleader, front and center—and the jazz vocal group. There'd been such energy in the gym, all the kids, Jeannie included, counting down the minutes and seconds until the final bell and the blessed freedom of a summer with no school.

For Jeannie and the rest of her class, it had been the final bell on high school. There'd be a formal graduation ceremony at the city's events center the following week, but the assembly was the last hurrah in the school itself for all the seniors. She'd been elated but she'd been nervous too. High school was a familiar routine, and there was comfort in the familiar. Everything post-graduation was like a yawning chasm filled with an unknowable future. Jeannie's future had turned out wonderfully, at least until this last year, but she hadn't known that then.

Standing in her old gym, even more than wandering the mostly deserted halls, was a step back into the familiar comfort of high school. She hadn't gone to any of her class's previous reunions. Why would she? She didn't need that kind of comfort. She'd made her own with her marriage to Jake. But now she understood why so many of her classmates went to reunion after reunion. High school had been the good old days, all their old experiences tinged with the golden glow of nostalgia.

It seemed surreal, especially since the gym didn't look like it had at that last assembly. The reunion committee had done a pretty good job of decorating the cavernous space to make it look fit for a Christmas dance. A huge sign hung on the cinderblock back wall welcoming the graduating class of 1998. More red, green, and white helium-filled balloons and crepe paper streamers seemed to hang from every available place. Round tables with butcher paper tablecloths and folding metal chairs were scattered across the gym floor. The overhead lights had been turned down to a semi-intimate setting, and a huge Christmas tree had been set up off to one side of the gym blocking off the entrance to the girls' locker room. The tree looked like it had been decorated by professionals. Jeannie wondered if someone on the reunion committee had gone into interior design.

Someone had set up a more than decent sound system, no mean feat considering the way sound bounced off the cinderblock walls and the wooden floor. She still remembered how horribly sound had echoed during basketball games. The sound had been a little better during school assemblies, but attendance at assemblies was required and all those bodies squeezed into the bleachers had acted as sound buffers. The basketball games had never really drawn big crowds. Jeannie had only gone to a few games herself, and only when Marta had a rare case of school spirit. Or she had a crush on one of the basketball players and wouldn't admit it.

A soulful rendition of a traditional Christmas carol by Boyz II Men was currently providing background music to all the various conversations going on around her. People were dancing to the Boyz in an empty space near the center of the gym that served as a dance floor.

Jeannie couldn't remember the size of her graduating class, but it seemed like at least half of them were in the gym, along with their significant others, of course. The tables were crowded and so was the dance floor. The three bartenders, Jimmy Jones included, were busy serving drinks, but Jimmy seemed to be taking a little longer than necessary mixing hers while he kept giving her looks that were dangerously close to a leer.

All three bartenders were dressed as Santa, minus the bushy white beards. She couldn't recall knowing Jimmy in high school. Then again, teenage Jimmy probably hadn't been able to fill out a Santa suit with his own belly. The years had apparently been very good to the former chess club president.

"Here you go," he said.

He handed her a plastic cup—red, of course. When their fingers briefly touched, he gave her an exaggerated wink, along with another one of the unsexist leers she'd ever seen.

"Thank you," she said. Her return smile was polite but nothing more. She didn't want to encourage him.

He didn't take the hint. "Maybe I'll run into you later?" he said. He nodded toward the other two bartenders. "Once these two can handle it on their own, we could have a dance or two." He waggled his eyebrows suggestively.

Jeannie sighed inwardly.

Maybe because she was one of the few unattached women at the reunion, she'd been hit on by most of the unattached men she'd run into so far. She'd only been at the reunion for a half hour or so, and warm fuzzy nostalgic feelings about being back in her old high school or not, she was beginning to regret her decision to come.

"I might have to leave shortly," she said. "I'm waiting for a phone call."

It was a little white lie, something she hated to do, but she wanted to let him down gently. She really didn't want to hurt his feelings. Still, she saw the disappointment on his face. She supposed she could be nice—it would be just one dance, after all—but she didn't feel like dancing with anyone. She hadn't gone anywhere like this by herself since Jake died, and she was missing him so much it wasn't funny.

She gave Jimmy another smile, this one a little more than just polite but, she hoped, not at all encouraging, and turned away from the bar to look at the huge Christmas tree. So different from the tree she and Jake used to put up, and far different from the tree she'd set up with Kristen the weekend before.

Kristen's tree was a little thing, barely four feet tall. Kristen had retrieved the boxes of holiday decorations from her garage, and she'd streamed holiday music on her cell phone the whole time they worked on the tree. Even though they were both dressed in lightweight summer-time clothes, the tree and the decorations and the music had made the afternoon feel festive.

A few days after Thanksgiving, Kristen had surprised Jeannie with a special holiday blend from her favorite coffee company. They'd brewed a pot while they worked. It wasn't quite the same as baking Christmas cookies like they'd done together when Kristen had been little, but the house had still been filled with the rich aroma of fresh-brewed coffee spiced with cinnamon, vanilla, and almonds.

The reunion's Christmas tree was grand, full of lights

and oversized ornaments in silver and gold and wrapped with wide ribbon garland, but Jeannie would take Kristen's little tree any day. The ornaments on her daughter's tree meant something to their family. Homemade ornaments they'd picked up at craft shows hung next to faded construction paper ornaments Kristen had made in grade school. Kristen even had the ornament Jeannie and Jake had given her the year she'd graduated high school—a little mouse in a cap and gown holding a candy-cane striped diploma.

The huge tree that blocked off the entrance to the girls' locker room reminded Jeannie of the trees she used to see whenever she and Jake went to holiday parties thrown by his clients. Those events had been professionally decorated, lavishly catered, and politically correct, but devoid of any real holiday spirit.

She took a sip of her drink. She didn't intend to drink much of it. She just wanted a drink to hold so that no one would offer to buy her one. In her experience—and granted, she'd had very little since she'd married Jake shortly after high school—a man who offered to buy a woman a drink expected her to spend a little time with him. And while she had no objections to having a conversation with someone, she'd been hit on so much already tonight she was beginning to doubt that any type of actual conversation would be happening.

At least she hadn't spotted any mistletoe among the rest of the decorations, and she'd really looked. She really, *really* didn't want some random stranger to kiss her and claim it was just tradition.

She had no idea why men who surely didn't remember her any more than she remembered them were so attracted to her. She wasn't the prettiest woman at the reunion, especially not with her hair trying to outdo itself in the frizz department thanks to her old hometown's familiar humidity. The prize for prettiest woman at the reunion went to Cissy, former head cheerleader. Cissy still had the same thin, lithe figure she'd had in high school. She was wearing a gorgeous red sequined party dress and had a little Santa hat pinned to her short blonde hair.

Cissy had enveloped Jeannie in an enthusiastic hug moments after Jeannie checked in at the reception table set up just outside the entrance to the gym. Cissy had peered at Jeannie's nametag, making no effort to disguise that she was reading Jeannie's name. That was no surprise. Cissy had totally ignored her in high school, and Jeannie doubted Cissy would have noticed her now if they passed each other on the street. Still, she'd hugged Jeannie hard like they'd been friends forever and thanked her for coming.

Jeannie had been so shocked, she hadn't even hugged Cissy back. Cissy didn't seem to mind. She just said she hoped Jeannie enjoyed herself.

It had been the same way once Jeannie made her way into the gym.

Women who hadn't given her the time of day in high school peered at her nametag, then gave her a huge hug and thanked her for coming.

"For Cissy," most of them had said.

Why Cissy? Because she was the chair of the reunion committee? Or because she'd been the head cheerleader? Did the old high school cliques never really go away? That was actually a rather depressing thought.

Jeannie was tempted to put her drink down on the bar and leave. Between the way women who were virtual strangers had embraced her, the way unattached men had been flirting with her, and the sheer number of people at the reunion—more people than she'd been around in ages—she was feeling more than a little overwhelmed. And if she was being honest with herself, the reunion was starting to depress her.

It wasn't just the fact that no one seemed to want to have a real conversation with her. And it wasn't the fact that if she wanted to dance, she'd have to dance with a stranger when the only person she'd danced with in nearly twenty-four years had been Jake.

She missed him, plain and simple. If he'd been here with her, she wouldn't feel so all alone. She hated to think of herself as someone who needed a man to complete her—she hoped she was more self-reliant than that—but maybe all these months of living with her daughter hadn't been an entirely good thing. What if she'd gotten too used to relying on someone else? Even though Kristen was busy most of the time with work and classes, the knowledge that she was still *there*, right there, if Jeannie needed her was just postponing the inevitable. Sooner or later she was going to have to learn how to live by herself. Learn that the person she needed to rely on was herself.

She wished she could talk with Jake about what she should do next, and that was a bad sign. *She* needed to decide what to do with her life now. Yes, she could discuss her plans with Kristen, but as the saying went, the buck now stopped entirely with Jeannie.

So if Kristen was right, if Jeannie had been hiding out in Arizona in a manner of speaking, the next logical step really was to move out on her own. Kind of the reverse of empty nest syndrome—she'd be the one to leave instead of her college-age daughter.

Then the question became where should she go?

Should she actually move back to her old hometown? Go somewhere familiar to start the next part of her life, the life of a middle-aged widow?

After her flight had landed the day before, she'd taken some time to drive her rental car around town. The place had grown in the last quarter century. New apartment complexes and a new mall expanded the town to the south. The mall looked like an upscale place, complete with an IMAX theater and an indoor ice skating rink. She'd almost gotten lost driving through new neighborhoods that hadn't existed when she and Jake moved to California. Thank goodness for the GPS app on her cell.

The downtown area had undergone a facelift, but the art store where she and Marta had spent way too much time (and far too much money) was still there. So was the mom-and-pop restaurant where her parents liked to go eat on Friday nights. Her mom had always ordered fish and chips, although she'd shared the fries with Jeannie's dad. Her dad had tried different things on the menu—experimenting with his taste buds, he'd said—but he always came back to the restaurant's chicken fried steak smothered in country gravy. Jeannie's favorite had been a BLT with a fruit cup on the side.

Funny, she couldn't remember now the last time she'd had a BLT. Even before she'd moved in with Kristen, who thought bacon was the ultimate dietary evil, Jeannie hadn't made herself a BLT or ordered one in a restaurant in years. How things changed.

Some things didn't. The 7-Eleven where she'd gone with Marta for early morning coffee was still there. It even looked like it still had the same tired posters in the windows. The hot dogs rotating on those hot metal rollers were probably cousins to the petrified ones Jeannie had wrinkled her nose at back in high school.

But the 7-Eleven across the street from where Kristen's friend Beth had lived was gone now, replaced with a modern gas station and mini-mart. And Jeannie hadn't seen a single Dairy Queen, which had given her an irrational craving for a soft-serve ice cream cone dipped in chocolate.

She'd felt a small punch in the gut when she'd driven down the street where she and Jake had leased their first house. Jake had been making decent money as a financial consultant—one of the honest ones who didn't get in trouble with the government—and their house had been a comfortable mid-size home in a neighborhood of cookie-cutter houses.

Now their house was gone. All the houses on the

block where they'd lived were gone. In their place was a modern apartment building, a U-shaped three-story monstrosity that had absolutely no artistic appeal whatsoever.

She was almost afraid to drive by the house where she'd grown up, but in the end she'd wanted to know. She breathed a small sigh of relief when she discovered that the house was still there. The yard wasn't well cared for, which would have upset her dad. He'd made a second career (it seemed) of caring for that plot of land. When the house had been their family home the lawn had been green, the shrubs neatly trimmed, and her dad had planted flowers in the red brick planters in front of the house throughout the year so that something was always in bloom. Now half the lawn had been dug up and replaced with uneven patio blocks. The brick planters in front of the house were overgrown with weeds, and the house itself was badly in need of a paint job.

Still, there were areas in town where the houses were moderately sized, and she'd seen For Sale signs in a few yards. Any one of those houses was something that a single woman could live in comfortably, and most of the yards were neat and not overgrown or ratty looking.

She hadn't made a note of any of the addresses of the houses for sale. She hadn't been ready yesterday to think about whether or not she might actually consider moving back here. Tonight, sipping a drink by herself while trying to avoid the advances of Jimmy Jones, Chess Club President, and coming to terms—finally—with the fact that she needed to find a new place to live, she thought it might be a good idea to arrange to tour some of those houses.

She was so engrossed in her thoughts that she never heard someone come up behind her.

"Didn't I tell you never to order a mixed drink in a bar?" came a familiar voice. "Bottled drinks you watch the bartender open, girlfriend."

Jeannie whirled around, nearly spilling her drink.

Marta stood behind her, as bold as day.

A warm feeling wrapped itself around Jeannie's heart like a comfortable blanket.

She couldn't believe it. Marta was actually here!

This reunion might be looking up after all.

CHAPTER 8

As promised, a limo picked Raymond up at six o'clock the next night.

The evening had been cool and damp enough that he'd covered his shiny new bell pepper green suit with a conservative tan raincoat. Lucas shouldn't complain too much. Once they got inside the high school, Raymond would have to take the raincoat off, so he'd still be displaying Lucas's handiwork.

The suit might be a hideous color, but it certainly fit like a glove. A well-worn, comfortable glove. Raymond had to admit that the green of the suit and the burgundy shirt worked well together, but he still felt like an overgrown elf on his way to a formal dance at the North Pole.

After the limo picked Raymond up, the driver stopped at Lucas's condo. When Lucas climbed in the back, Raymond's mouth dropped open. He couldn't help it.

Lucas hadn't lied—he'd given Raymond the more

conservative of the two suits. The shiny burgundy red jacket and pants Lucas was wearing made him look like a plate of jellied cranberry sauce, and the green shirt and pocket square looked more like mint jelly than bell peppers. Instead of dress shoes, Lucas wore fancy dress boots the same burgundy color as the suit. To top it off, he was wearing a cape—an actual cape—made of the same shiny green material as Raymond's suit, only the cape had gold threads running through it, much like Raymond's tie.

As a final touch, Lucas had on green-rimmed glasses and green leather gloves.

"You look like Elton John paid a visit to Santa's tailor," Raymond said.

Lucas smiled at him. "That's exactly the look I was going for." He gave Raymond a critical once-over. "You look fabulous, by the way. Except for the overcoat."

Raymond fought not to roll his eyes. He didn't want to look fabulous. He wanted to spend the minimum amount of time necessary at the reunion to sufficiently show off Lucas's festive holiday duds, and then go home and change into something comfortable.

Something out of his own closet.

The limo driver got back behind the wheel and pulled into traffic.

Lucas leaned back in his seat. "The bar in this beast is fully stocked, by the way. Just in case you need a little liquid fortitude before we brave the denizens of the suburbs, otherwise known as my old classmates."

Raymond shook his head. The last thing he needed

tonight was to drink too much. In fact, he might not drink at all. At most functions he limited himself to one cocktail to be polite, and half the time he didn't finish that. If he thought of tonight as a professional function, he'd be able to deal with whatever came at him.

With any luck.

Today he'd decorated his house for Christmas. He'd hoped it would help put him in the holiday spirit, but that had only been partly successful. He'd talked to Marri on the phone in the morning. Like all calls with his daughter, he'd mostly listened while she rattled on about something that happened on her favorite cartoon that morning, and how excited she was that it was almost Christmas but that it was taking so long to get here, and was he sure that Santa would know to leave her presents at his house instead of Mommy's?

He'd assured her that Santa knew exactly where all the good little boys and girls would be on Christmas. When she'd asked if she was one of Santa's good little girls, such uncertainty had flooded her voice that it nearly broke his heart.

"Of course, sweetheart," he'd said. "Never doubt that."

"Are you sure?"

"Absolutely," he'd said. "Why are you even worried about that?"

She hadn't say anything for long enough he'd wondered whether she'd put down the phone and wandered off. That had happened before when she was younger, but not so much now that she was a big girl of six.

"I think I made Mommy mad," she'd finally said. She might as well have been fessing up to stealing all the cookies out of the cookie jar, her voice was so subdued and sad.

With a little careful questioning—he didn't want to upset her any more than she already was—he'd managed to get enough of the story that he could fill in the blanks.

Belinda had been griping to her husband about Marri going to his house for Christmas. As usual with Belinda, whenever she started really complaining about something, all the little imagined slights and frustrations she'd suffered months and months ago came pouring out. Marri had caught just enough of the tirade to think that she was the cause of all her mommy's problems.

Belinda hadn't helped the matter when she'd caught Marri listening. She'd sent Marri to her room, which to Marri's mind meant she was in trouble. Raymond was sure Belinda hadn't meant it that way—she probably just didn't want Marri listening in while her mommy ranted about life in general and Raymond (he was sure he featured prominently in Belinda's complaints)—but to a six-year-old, being sent to her room meant she was in trouble.

"You know what I think?" Raymond said after his daughter had finished her story.

"No." Her voice was still so soft and heartbroken that his own heart ached.

"I think Mommy must have been having a bad day.

Sometimes adults have bad days and they have to talk their feelings out so they can feel better."

"Do you have bad days, Daddy?"

Did he? He'd had a bad one on Thanksgiving, but he wasn't about to tell her that.

"Not when you're with me, cuddle bug," he said instead.

She'd actually giggled, which made him feel a little better. Right up until the call ended and he'd looked around his house and realized he hadn't done anything to make it ready to host a little girl on Christmas Day.

So he'd hauled all the old decorations down from the attic. Belinda hadn't taken any of their holiday décor, as she'd called it, when she left. The first time he'd picked up Marri on Christmas Day, he'd discovered that his ex had bought all new decorations. All of it looked like she'd picked it out of one of the magazines she continually studied to learn about new trends in interior design. Her decorations were gorgeous and perfectly placed and felt as cold as a damp winter night.

He'd always preferred the mishmash of things they'd collected over the years. A handblown glass ornament they'd found at a craft show the first year they'd been married. A silly penguin holding a Christmas stocking stuffed with fake money he'd been given by his office staff after the agency had posted its first million dollar year. A silver frame ornament with a picture of baby Marri and the caption *Baby's First Christmas.*

The Christmas tree was an artificial blue spruce. He set it up in the window at the front corner of the living room so the tree could be seen from the street. More importantly, where Marri could see the tree as she ran up his front steps. He put all the old ornaments on it, and then strung lights around the window.

He strung more lights outside, following the pattern he'd used for years. It certainly made the yard and his house feel a little more like Christmas, but would Marri like it? Maybe he should look for holiday decorations featuring her favorite cartoon characters. It was a pretty popular show, from what his assistant told him. He should be able to find something new that would be Marri's and hers alone, and more importantly, something that she could keep at his house.

Right before he got dressed for the reunion, he made a note on his calendar to go shopping on Monday morning to look for things for Marri that could stay at his house. She was getting old enough now that she needed to feel like she belonged in a house that had increasingly started to feel—to him, anyway—like a place a single man lived, but didn't really live *in*. And while he was a single man, he was also a single father, and his house should reflect that his daughter lived there too.

The Christmas decorations were a good start, but they were only temporary. Come New Year's Day, he'd be packing them away again in the attic. He needed things she could call her own that would stay out year round.

He'd been making a mental list during the limo ride to pick up Lucas. Even after he'd declined to raid the limo's liquor supply, he was still trying to think of things his little girl would both need and like, and wouldn't spoil her—too much.

Lucas gave him a quizzical look. "You haven't heard a word I said. It's like you're a million miles away."

"Guess I am," Raymond said. He explained what he'd decided to do for Marri. "The problem is that she was only two when we split up," he said. "She spends almost all her time at Belinda's, so I never even thought she might want things of her own to keep at my house."

To his credit, Lucas didn't brush off Raymond's concerns even though he was probably nervous about what kind of reception he'd get at the reunion. "What brought this on today?"

Raymond thought about it. It wasn't that Marri had suddenly been concerned that she wasn't a good girl.

It was that she automatically thought Santa would look for her at Belinda's house. In six-year-old terms, that meant she considered Belinda's house her home. His house was only someplace she visited, and not all that often.

When Raymond told Lucas that, his cousin looked thoughtful. "It's not just things that make a house a home, you know," he said. "I've never been the settle down type, but you, dear cousin, are a family man without a family. You've let Belinda browbeat you into a position where you only get to be an occasional dad. Today your daughter hit you with a clue-by-four, but that's only part of the problem."

"And what's the rest of my problem?"

Raymond didn't really want to know, but Lucas would tell him whether Raymond asked or not.

"You're lonely," Lucas said.

Before Raymond could protest that while he was many things, lonely wasn't one of them, Lucas held up a hand to stop him.

"You've convinced yourself this is the way your life is supposed to be now, but this fabulous gay man is telling you that you need someone else to come home to at night besides a microwave meal-in-a-box." He looked at Raymond over the top of his glasses. "And yes, I know a microwave meal isn't a some*one*, but I'm sure I don't need to spell it out for you."

Get back in the saddle. Back on the horse. On the bike.

Raymond had heard all the cute little sayings, some from well-meaning friends, some from office staff until he'd glared at them and told them enough was enough. That he was a grown man and could decide for himself when he wanted to start dating again.

If he wanted to start dating again.

Lucas put a hand on Raymond's knee. "It's been long enough," he said. "You don't have to be alone because you're a daddy, you know. You can be a daddy *and* someone who dates."

Raymond knew Lucas wouldn't drop the subject until Raymond agreed with him. And besides, what Lucas had said actually struck a nerve. Belinda had moved on. She might have moved on even before they'd decided to divorce. But he'd been stuck trying to wrap his head around being single again when he'd expected to be married for the rest of his life. Of not having his daughter with him every night after he came home from work. He hadn't been mentally prepared for that, so he'd thrown himself in other things, like building up his agency, but at least he still spent time with his daughter on a regular basis.

Then Belinda had remarried and got a judge to agree that she could take Marri with her when she moved to Tacoma. That was just far enough away to keep him from spending more than a few days a month with his daughter.

That had been another adjustment. Another reason to put off trying to date, because one thing he'd learned about himself was that he couldn't do casual relationships. The kind that were all about sex but had nothing to do with building an actual connection with someone else. He'd tried dating women he knew weren't interested in a lasting relationship, but those brief encounters always left him feeling empty inside.

What had Lucas said? That he was a family man without a family? That was actually a pretty accurate description.

"You might have a point," he said. "But I think I'll table the whole looking for Ms. Right until after the first of the year."

It was an off-the-cuff remark meant just to appease his cousin. Even if he was serious, Raymond knew he probably wouldn't be able to connect with anyone until then anyway. Most of the people he knew who might be able to introduce him to someone he had even a remote chance of being interested in and who'd be interested in *him* were busy with their own holiday plans. And he was pretty sure he wouldn't meet anyone at the reunion who'd be willing to give him a chance.

Not while he was dressed like he was part of a gay power couple.

He really should have said no to the suit.

He cut his eyes to the liquor cabinet. "Have any sparkling water in there?" he asked.

Lucas raised an eyebrow. "Just water? Nothing stronger?"

"Not now," Raymond said. "Ask me in an hour."

He might need one by then.

CHAPTER 9

Jeannie couldn't believe it. Marta was actually at the reunion!

"Surprised you, didn't I?" Marta said.

Jeannie put her drink down on the bar and enveloped Marta in a huge hug. "You could have told me," she said.

Marta laughed. "And miss the look on your face? Not in a million years."

All around them, couples were dancing and clustered together in little conversation groups. Thanks to the crowd noise and raucous laughter from people who'd had more than a few drinks by now, plus an old rock version of a Christmas carol playing over the sound system, Jeannie felt she had to shout to make herself heard.

She didn't care. After more than twenty years, she was holding her best friend in her arms and she never wanted to let her go. This hug, this feeling—that's what had been missing from the reunion. From her entire trip back home.

Feeling like she belonged.

Eventually Marta patted Jeannie on the back and gave her a quick kiss to the shoulder. "I know," she murmured. "It'll get better."

Marta had said almost the exact same thing during their first conversation after Jake died. And it had gotten better. But hearing it now whispered against her shoulder brought pinpricks of tears to Jeannie's eyes.

The last thing she wanted to do was cry in front of a bunch of strangers, so she ended the hug and gave Marta a mock glare.

"You lied to me," she said. "You told me you weren't coming!"

Marta gave her a rueful smile. "I know. I kept it a secret, but it wasn't really a lie at the time. I didn't think I could afford it, but then I sold a few pieces and *voila!* Here I am."

Marta's art must go for a pretty penny. Last-minute cross-country flights weren't cheap. Jeannie had been appalled at how expensive her own airline tickets had been.

"You look pretty good for an old fart," Marta said, giving Jeannie the once over. "You on an exercise kick or something?"

Marta still looked the same. Still slightly heavier than conventional wisdom said was ideal. Still dressed in black, this time in a swirling, full-length black skirt, sequined black blouse cut low enough to show her ample cleavage, and black lace-up boots. Her hair was still long and black and straight, with thick bangs covering her forehead. She'd accented her hair with electric red metallic extensions that sparkled even in the dim light of the gym.

Jeannie, on the other hand, had dressed conservatively. She wore her new dark blue linen slacks and one of her favorite light-weight sweaters, this one a dusty lavender with a wide, angled collar and three-quarter length sleeves. She'd considered wearing a Christmas sweater she'd packed for the trip, but at the last minute decided on something not holiday related in case the reunion ignored the holiday season. She shouldn't have worried.

The sweater was a lot looser than the last time she'd worn it, but it was a comfortable kind of loose, not a baggy, you're wearing your older sister's hand-me-downs loose.

"My daughter's fault," Jeannie said. She explained how Kristen was training for a marathon and had totally changed her eating habits.

"I eat like an artist who still thinks she's starving," Marta said. "Only now I get my ramen from this place in the Village that puts that cheap old stuff I used to eat to shame."

Jeannie had done the ramen thing briefly back when Jake was still getting started in business. She'd dressed up the cheap ramen noodle soup with fresh vegetables and bits of chicken left over from a roast she made every

Sunday. It hadn't been half bad. It hadn't been half good either.

"The good old, bad old days, right?" she said.

"That's what reunions are all about," Marta said. "Reminiscing about the good old times. Checking out who got married, who has kids. Who had an affair with what used car salesman. Speaking of... did Cissy give you a hug? I thought she'd break my ribs. What's up with that?"

Jeannie shrugged. "She did the same thing to me. I didn't think she even remembered me. You, she'd remember."

"I always thought she hated my guts," Marta said. "I was the weird goth chick with no school spirit. Kind of the anti-Cissy. Yet tonight she acted like we'd always been besties."

Marta put a singsong emphasis on *besties*. It was a pretty good Valley Girl imitation.

Another Christmas song came over the sound system —Madonna's "Santa Baby."

"They've been playing that kind of thing all night?" Marta asked.

Jeannie gestured at the huge Christmas tree. "It's a theme, which I guess makes sense if you're going to hold a reunion in December."

"I told you, the suburbs melted their brains."

"I live in the suburbs," Jeannie said.

Marta waved her hand in a never-mind gesture. "You live in Arizona. You probably have cactus instead of lawns. That doesn't count."

Jeannie wondered if Kristen would agree with that.

"Hey," Marta said. "Do you remember the time Scooter McClennon got ahold of that weird holiday CD? The one where all the lyrics to the songs had been changed? And he played it over the intercom?"

Every class had to have a class clown. Scooter McClennon had held that title in Marta and Jeannie's graduating class. He told jokes at school assemblies that were just this side of being too over-the-line for the school administrators to allow. He played tuba in the band and from what Jeannie had heard, played the stripper song in the band room whenever the instructor was late for class. Which apparently had been a fairly common occurrence.

But Scooter's crowning achievement their senior year had been when he played Bob Rivers' Twisted Christmas version of "God Rest Ye Merry Gentlemen" over the school's intercom system.

Rivers' parody of the old Christmas classic had something to do with a guy going into the wrong restroom and being traumatized for life. Scooter had managed to broadcast almost the entire song before the intercom abruptly cut out amid much shouting and Scooter's maniacal laughter. He'd gotten a day's suspension, which he said he spent lounging around his house and eating Christmas cookies.

"That was actually pretty funny," Jeannie said. "Remember Mrs. Trotter? How she tried to act all scandalized, but I could have sworn she had a glint in her eye."

Jeannie and Marta had both been in Mrs. Trotter's Popular Literature class at the time. It had been the most fun English Department class ever. Instead of reading novels written a couple hundred years ago, they read modern novels in a wide variety of genres. Mrs. Trotter said she wanted to instill in her students a lifelong habit of reading for fun, instead of viewing reading as a chore.

"Mrs. Trotter thought our principal had a stick up his butt," Marta said. "She never told any of us, but I overheard her talking to one of the other teachers once. Said she thought the guy should loosen up a bit before he gave himself a heart attack." She gave Jeannie a wicked grin. "I think she smoked pot on the weekends."

Jeannie had been horribly naïve when she'd first started high school. That had changed when she'd become friends with Marta in her sophomore year. She'd had a hard time thinking of her old high school teachers as anything except teachers. Even now she couldn't imagine Mrs. Trotter lighting up just to mellow herself out enough to put up with a bunch of high school students.

"You think he's here tonight?" Marta asked. "Good old Scooter?"

Jeannie looked around the gym. It wasn't easy to see much of anything over the press of bodies on the dance floor. Not that she'd know what Scooter looked like these days.

She didn't see anyone who looked like he might be Scooter. She was about to tell Marta that when her gaze was caught by a handsome gay couple dressed in coordinating holiday suits walking through the balloon-covered trellis at the entrance to the gym.

Jeannie narrowed her eyes. The shorter of the two men looked vaguely familiar.

She couldn't remember his name, but one of the students in their graduating class had been the most flamboyantly gay kid in their rather conservative school. Jeannie had been ignored for the most part in high school. He'd been tormented. Which meant that Marta, being the contrarian she was, had befriended him.

"Isn't that your friend—" she began, but Marta interrupted her with a loud shout.

"Lucas!"

Marta's voice carried over the music. Half the people on the dance floor turned to look at them. Marta didn't seem to mind, of course.

The man Marta had shouted at looked in her direction. A huge grin split his face.

"Marta-farta!" he shouted back, waving one arm frantically.

Jeannie couldn't help but notice that the man Lucas was with looked as though he wanted to sink into the floor. If he was dating someone as flamboyant as Lucas—and their coordinating suits certainly made it look as if they'd been dating for a while, if they weren't an actual couple—he should be used to things like this by now.

Marta made a beeline toward Lucas and his friend.

Jeannie grabbed her drink from the bar and trailed along in Marta's wake. She'd gone from being alone and miserable at the reunion to now looking like she'd be part of a group, and a small one at that. Just the way she liked it.

Yes, indeed. The evening was definitely looking up.

CHAPTER 10

*M*arta-farta?

Raymond felt like covering his face with his hands to cover what he was sure was a blush that rivaled the color of Lucas's suit and his own shirt.

It was bad enough that he'd gotten knowing looks from the women at the registration table who'd checked them in. He'd given his overcoat to one of them to check in, along with Lucas's cape, while the other had hand-written his name on a nametag. Both women had assumed Raymond was more than Lucas's plus one.

The suits. It was the matching suits that did it. Casual acquaintances didn't wear custom-made coordinating suits. Everyone was making the assumption that Raymond was Lucas's actual romantic date. And while Raymond had thought he wouldn't mind if relative strangers believed the two of them were dating, he actually knew Marta—sort of.

Back during Lucas's high school days, she'd been over

at his house a few times when Raymond and his mom had been there. Raymond had thought Marta was an interesting person. Not in a potential date kind of way, but she was so unique and self-assured—and she always had Lucas's back, from what Lucas said—that it was impossible not for Raymond to like her.

At least, that's the way it had been for him. According to Lucas, Marta hadn't been all that well-liked in high school. It was one of the things that had made them friends.

Lucas was acting now like seeing her was a total surprise. Raymond knew that his cousin had lost track of her after high school, so maybe she'd moved away and Lucas didn't know she'd be coming to the reunion. Raymond decided to go with that assumption since it meant he wouldn't have to give Lucas grief for getting him to wear this ridiculous suit in front of someone he actually knew.

He'd just never heard Lucas use that nickname for her before. And now he'd shouted it loud enough for everyone to hear, which meant half the people in the gym had turned around to stare at them.

And there were a whole lot of people in the gym. More than Raymond had expected for a high school reunion two weeks before Christmas. Now that Lucas had announced their presence, Raymond wouldn't be able to hang out on the sidelines while Lucas did his fabulously successful gay man thing. Most of the people here were going to think the two of them were a couple.

Unless he wanted to be miserable all night, he should probably just relax and enjoy it.

He hadn't been to Parker High since his own high school days. Half the football players had also been on the basketball team. Raymond had played in away games here, and he'd gone to a few basketball games to support his buddies. They'd always sat on the wooden bleachers, which were currently folded up against the wall. Thank goodness no one expected anyone attending the reunion to climb the bleachers, much less sit on those wooden seats. People who'd graduated twenty-four years ago weren't exactly decrepit, but unless they were still athletic, sitting on wooden seats all night wouldn't do them any good.

The gym had looked bigger in the days when he'd come to the games, but he supposed everyone who went back to their own high school felt that the place had shrunk.

The people in charge of the reunion had run with the Christmas theme. There was a huge Christmas tree off to one corner strategically placed in front of the entrance to the girls' locker room. The overhead fluorescents had been dimmed, and there were enough balloons and streamers in Christmas colors to put the fanciest prom he'd been to during his own high school years to shame.

There was a bar, of course, and from the size of the crowd around the bar, the reunion was doing a bang-up job of keeping attendees well-supplied with drinks. Back in the limo he'd told Lucas that he might want a drink later. If he was going to pull off being okay with the assumption he and his cousin were dating, he might need that drink right about now.

Lucas met Marta at the border between an area filled with tables and the space in the middle of the gym where couples were dancing to Christmas music. The two of them enveloped each other in a bear hug. For a minute, Raymond thought Lucas might lift her off the floor, but she was actually the taller of the two by a couple of inches. Lucas must have decided if either of them was going to lift the other up, it should be Marta.

She didn't, but from where Raymond stood watching, it looked like a close call.

He couldn't remember ever seeing his cousin quite so happy. Lucas might play the field, never really letting any of the men he dated get close to him, but Raymond always thought that deep down inside, Lucas was a lonely man. As far as Raymond knew, Lucas had no close friends who weren't business acquaintances.

Look who's talking, Raymond told himself. He had his work buddies—real estate agents and brokers who worked for other firms—but there was always a bit of quiet competition in those friendships. The few women he'd had friendships with over the years had gone their separate ways, either into romantic relationships that left little time for anything else, or they'd moved away.

Was he really as lonely as Lucas had accused him of being?

His train of thought derailed when he caught sight of the woman trailing after Marta. She was petite, but not in a delicate way, with dark hair that framed her face perfectly.

His initial thought was that she was cute, which was an odd thing to say about a woman who had to be close to his own age.

Then she got close enough that he could really see her in the dim light in the gym.

She took his breath away. It was as simple as that. She was the most beautiful woman he'd seen in a long, long time.

So of course, he'd have to meet her while he was wearing a shiny green suit that made him look like an overgrown Christmas elf.

She held out her hand and introduced herself as Jeannie Carlson. "Do you know Marta too?"

He took her hand, smooth and soft but with an underlying strength. He intended to introduce himself, but as soon as his fingers touched her skin, he felt a spark. An actual spark, and it startled him.

Had he ever felt something like that before? He couldn't remember. He certainly hadn't felt it with his ex-wife.

Her eyes widened just the slightest. Had she felt something too?

"Raymond Ellis," he said, belatedly remembering that she was waiting for his name.

He was still holding her hand. Whatever it was he'd felt, he didn't want to let go of that feeling. But he was more than half a foot taller than she was. He didn't want to come off like some creep who was looming over her, so he reluctantly let go.

Then he remembered that she'd asked him a question about whether he knew Marta.

"Not really," he said. "Not the way Lucas does."

She smiled at him. The smile lit up her whole face. "I take it he doesn't call people 'farta' all the time."

Raymond smiled back. "Not that I've heard."

"It was one of his tamer nicknames for her."

She went on to not only tell him some of the other wildly inappropriate nicknames Lucas had called Marta, but also to tell him the reasons behind the most imaginative ones.

Raymond was totally engrossed. She could have been reading MLS listings to him, and he would have been just as fascinated. Her voice was soothing with just a hint of a rasp. She had no accent as far as he could tell. She was also clearly one of Lucas's classmates. Did she still live in the area? And if she did, why hadn't Lucas ever mentioned her?

She abruptly quit telling him about the story behind one of Lucas's high school shenanigans, her expression suddenly unsure. He realized he'd just been standing there, staring at her like some lovesick schoolboy, and that he'd probably made her self-conscious.

Smooth move, buddy.

"I'm sorry," she said. "I really shouldn't be allowed out in public. It's been a while since I've been to any kind of social gathering. Here I've been babbling away, probably telling you things you already know. I should have asked you if you've known Lucas long."

"All his life," Lucas said, inserting himself into the conversation.

The marathon hug was apparently over, because Marta turned toward Raymond and swept him up in a hug that was no less enthusiastic than the one she'd given Lucas. Although it was much shorter in duration.

This was apparently the night for hugging. One of the women who'd been at the table outside the gym had given him a hug right after he'd stuck his nametag on his suit coat. He'd been surprised, and for a split second wondered if she was someone he should have recognized. Her nametag read "Cissy," and he didn't remember anyone named Cissy among Lucas's few friends.

Marta ended the hug. "Good to see you. You keeping my boy out of trouble?" she asked with a wicked glint in her eyes.

"You have seen our suits, right?" Raymond said. "What do you think?"

"I think he has a marvelous eye for color, but he always did." She glanced back and forth between him and her friend Jeannie. "You've already met?"

"We have," he said, unable to keep the grin off his face at the memory of how he'd felt holding Jeannie's hand.

"Jeannie and I were best buds," Marta said. "We told each other everything."

"Everything?" Jeannie said. "You never told me about Raymond."

"Some things are better kept secret," Lucas said, briefly putting one hand on Raymond's elbow. "My thirst is not one of them, and I see a bar. I think my plus-one and I should go get drinks while you girls find an open table."

"You just want to show off," Marta said.

Lucas gave her a happy smile along with an arch look over the top of his glasses. He was clearly in his element, now that Marta was here. It looked like this evening was actually off to a good start.

"You know me too well," Lucas told Marta. "But if I really wanted to show off, I would have kept on the cape."

"A cape?" Marta said.

"An actual cape," Raymond said, deciding to get a word in edgewise while he still could.

He glanced at Jeannie to see how she was taking Lucas in his full-on flamboyant mode. She had an amused expression on her face, and while she hadn't joined in the banter, she seemed to be enjoying herself.

Marta glanced back and forth between Raymond and her friend again. "Tell you what," she said, deftly taking Lucas's hand. "How about you and I go get the drinks. I know what Jeannie likes, and someone needs to protect you from the Santa bartenders. With that red suit, they might think you're an escaped elf."

"Oh, my," Lucas said. "My dark little raincloud is willing to brave the denizens of the bar with me?" He batted his eyelashes at her. "How could I resist?"

"I already have..." Jeannie started to say as Lucas peered at her barely touched drink. "It's diet."

"That's just nasty," he said. "Let's get you a proper drink, shall we?"

He started to lead Marta away, but she held up a finger in a wait-one-second gesture. She came back and whispered something in Jeannie's ear, then she was off with Lucas, arms linked together, her black skirt swirling around her ankles as they headed through the dancers toward the bar.

Raymond turned back to Jeannie, ready to pick up their conversation, but whatever he was about to say died on his lips.

She was blushing all the way from her neck to her hairline, which was odd enough. But what froze him to the spot was that she was looking at him like he was a ghost, and she was just about as happy to see him as Scrouge had been to see all his ghosts on Christmas Eve.

CHAPTER 11

Jeannie was mortified.

She'd been babbling away like an idiot, sharing all sorts of things about Lucas and his odd friendship with Marta, all while she'd been under the impression that Raymond was Lucas's date.

She tried to tell herself it was an honest mistake. Raymond was an incredibly handsome man. Tall with dark hair cut short but not *too* short, he had a strong jaw and cheekbones to die for. In the dim light of the gym, she hadn't been able to tell whether his eyes were dark blue or brown, but they looked kind. Just the kind of man who'd be a good foil for Lucas's flamboyance.

Yes, she'd felt a definite pull of attraction when he'd taken her hand, and yes, he'd held onto her hand just a few moments longer than strictly necessary, but she'd thought it was clear from their outfits that Raymond and Lucas were a couple. Would a straight man be caught out in public in a suit like that? Especially when it matched the one the gay man he was with was wearing?

She didn't think so, but apparently that was exactly the case.

"He's Lucas's cousin," Marta had whispered in her ear. "A couple of years older than we are. Divorced. Father of one. And definitely *not* gay."

Jeannie had been berating herself for being attracted to a gay man. She'd been startled by that zing of attraction when he'd held her hand. Attraction to a man was the last thing on her mind. She hadn't felt any sort of attraction toward anyone since Jake had passed away. In fact, she'd started to believe she'd never be attracted to another man again. So of *course,* she'd be attracted to someone totally unavailable because he was gay.

Only he wasn't.

And Marta had left her alone with him! Deliberately. She'd definitely had a Marta-*farta* glint in her eyes as she'd gone off to the bar with Lucas.

Jeannie wanted to disappear into the floor, she was so embarrassed. Which he could no doubt tell. Her face felt hot, which meant she was blushing all the way to the roots of her hair. Sometimes her fair complexion could be her worst enemy.

"Should we grab a table?" Raymond asked.

A table?

Jeannie blinked. Of course they'd need a table for when Marta and Lucas brought back drinks.

She glanced toward the bar. A small crowd had gathered around Marta and Lucas, but it looked like Lucas, at least, was holding his own. Maybe the old teenage dynamics really didn't apply anymore. Women who'd ignored Jeannie in high school were treating her like long-lost friends. Some of the men at the bar were probably the same people who'd bullied Lucas relentlessly in school, but now they were acting like they'd been friends all along.

"Look at that," Raymond said. She glanced at him, but he was looking toward the bar and grinning. "He's certainly in his element."

She studied his face while he watched his cousin. He seemed genuinely happy for Lucas. She might be mistaken, but she also thought she saw a bit of relief in his expression. He must have been worried about how Lucas would be received. From what she remembered, Lucas had been flamboyant in high school, but never *this* flamboyant.

"Is he always so..." She trailed off, not knowing how to put it without unintentionally saying something offensive.

"So Lucas?" Raymond turned his grin back on her. "No, he's dialed up to about eleven tonight. Usually he runs around seven or eight."

She nodded, but she didn't smile back, and his grin faded. Doubt started to cloud his expression.

"About that table?" he asked. "Should we find one, or do you have someone else you—"

"Oh. No." She didn't have anyone else she wanted to spend time with, but she was clearly giving that impression.

She made herself take a deep breath. He had been nothing but nice to her—in fact, now that she thought about it, he might have even been starting to flirt with her (if she could even recognize what flirting was after all these years)—and being embarrassed was all on her and her erroneous assumptions.

"Finding a table sounds wonderful," she said.

Then she berated herself for saying *wonderful*. She could have chosen a more neutral word, not one so over-the-top. *Nice* would have been a better word, or would that have sounded too formal? At least she hadn't said *awesome*.

She realized he was looking at her oddly. She'd missed whatever he'd said while she was mentally giving herself a hard time over a single word, just like she was an awkward teenager on a first date with a guy she had a crush on.

She hadn't even done that when she'd been a teenager.

She gave him a rueful smile. "I'm sorry. That didn't quite come out right. I'm terrible at this—flir...getting-to-know-you small talk."

Good grief. She'd almost said *flirting!* She really was out of practice.

"I probably shouldn't be allowed out in public," she added. "Can we just forget I said that?"

He chuckled. It was deep, rich sound, and while it wasn't loud, it still reached her over the music and the crowd noise and the beating of her heart, which still hadn't settled down.

"I'm here with Lucas, dressed like *this*," he said, gesturing at his suit, "and you have to ask if I'm okay with the occasional conversational gaffe?"

He seemed to wince, a brief flicker, barely there and gone.

Was he berating himself over *gaffe*? Marta had said he was divorced, but she hadn't said how recently. Maybe he was out of practice at this kind of small talk too.

That thought actually made her feel better, and the tight, nervous ball of embarrassment that had settled deep inside her turned into a much more pleasant type of excitement.

"So Lucas is your cousin?" she asked.

"Yeah. He asked me to be his plus-one so he wouldn't have to show up alone..." He trailed off. A lightbulb had probably gone off somewhere inside his brain, and Jeannie felt a blush start again. "You thought we were... that I was...?"

This time he looked embarrassed, and he didn't wait for her to answer.

"Of course, you would," he said. "I should have told him I'd only come if I could wear my own clothes, but I never thought he'd do something like this."

"Not your normal attire, I take it," she said.

"Oh, good lord, no. It's from Lucas's clothing line. He's a designer. A successful one, at least now. In high school, he was an outcast, but you probably know that."

"And you agreed to come along as moral support." That said a lot about his character, right there. Not a lot of straight men would agree to do something like that, no matter how much they loved their cousin.

Someone at a nearby table took a photo with their cell. The flash illuminated his face long enough to give her a good look at his eyes. They were the deepest blue. She found herself gazing at him just a little too long until the corners of his mouth quirked up in a grin. She grinned back. She thought she could look in those eyes for a long time. Even lose herself there, at least for a little while.

And the best part was that he seemed perfectly willing to gaze right back at her. Maybe they were actually flirting.

"Guess we should try to grab a table," he said. "Before they get back and we're still standing right where they left us."

She reluctantly broke their gaze. There was an empty table near the back, on the other side of the gym from the bar and the Christmas tree and most of the crowd.

"How about that one?" she asked, gesturing at the table.

"Lead on," he said.

The tables had been placed widely enough apart that they could walk side by side. He was just tall enough that she could glance up at him without having to glance up too far. Jake had been only a couple of inches taller than she was, and looking up at a man was a new experience, but not an unpleasant one.

"Did you come with Marta tonight?" he asked.

"I didn't even know she was coming," she said. "I was about to leave before she surprised me."

"Not having a good time?"

He had glanced down at her with something that looked like genuine concern.

No, she hadn't been having a good time. She'd been missing Jake and feeling all alone and lonely and regretting the decision to even make this trip. What had she been thinking? That she could just move back home, leave Kristen behind, start all over again and everything would be fine?

She still wasn't sure about moving back here and starting over. Those were decisions for another day. But at least she was no longer regretting her decision to come to the reunion.

Was she having a good time?

That she could answer.

"I am now," she said.

CHAPTER 12

By the time Raymond started on his second watered-down drink, he knew he was in trouble.

He was falling for a beautiful widow who lived with her daughter in Arizona.

They'd been talking and flirting—actually flirting, although he was woefully out of practice—for almost an hour. Lucas and Marta sat with them at times, and at other times they left to go show off Lucas's successful self to someone who used to torment him in high school. The two of them looked like they were having the time of their lives.

He was too, but a part of him was telling him he didn't need another complication in his life.

Jeannie lived in *Arizona*. Not exactly across the country, but not exactly next door either. He already had issues simply arranging with Belinda to spend time with his daughter, and his ex only lived in Tacoma. That was practically next door compared to the distance between Portland and Arizona.

What he really wanted to do was just relax and enjoy Jeannie's company. Not to be too concerned about where this relationship might be heading, or if it even could develop into a relationship. Jeannie was gorgeous, no doubt about that, and now that she'd gotten over her embarrassment at assuming he was gay and in a relationship with Lucas, she was incredibly easy to talk to. In fact, it felt like they'd known each other for years. She was funny and sweet and amazingly intelligent. She owned her own graphic design firm, a one-person operation she said she might need to expand since business had begun to pick up, but that was a decision she'd decided to put off until after the first of the year.

She even talked about her husband. She'd been widowed very suddenly in January, and admitted it had devastated her. "He was my first love," she said. "We had a wonderful twenty-three years together."

Raymond did the math in his head. She must have been married right out of high school.

"Did you go to school together?" he asked.

"Oh, no. He was a mature man of twenty-five." She grinned. "We were *so* young. We didn't know what we were getting into, and then Kristen came along and we still didn't know what we were doing. Thank goodness my parents were around to help."

Her parents had long since moved to Southern California. "They couldn't deal with the damp," she said. "Now mom complains about the heat, but I think they like it."

Raymond's parents had retired to New Hampshire, of all places. He talked to them often on Zoom, which his mom had been inordinately proud that she'd learned how to use. They always had at least one Zoom conversation whenever he had Marri. The way things were going in that part of his life, he supposed their next Zoom call with their granddaughter would be on Christmas Day.

He told her about his parents. About his marriage to Belinda, about how they'd all but given up on having kids until Marri came along.

"How old is your daughter?" Jeannie asked.

"A very mature six," he said, unintentionally echoing her description of her husband.

She lifted one perfectly shaped eyebrow and grinned at him. "And you have pictures, of course."

So he dug out his cell and thumbed through the embarrassingly large photo album of his daughter.

Jeannie seemed enthralled. She said she only had a few pictures of her daughter, which she shared. He was surprised to see a gorgeous young woman instead of a young teenager. Most of the people he knew who were his age and had children were all raising teenagers, many of them difficult teenagers. Then again, Jeannie had said she'd married young, but she still didn't look old enough to have a daughter in college.

They had their heads together, looking at pictures of

their children on their cell phones, when he realized this must be what dating was like for people his age. At least for people his age who were on their second relationship.

That's when he realized that he really was thinking about Jeannie in terms of a relationship. An actual relationship that might extend past tonight.

He'd been avoiding even a hint of a relationship ever since his divorce. The divorce had blindsided him. Not in the same way Jeannie's husband's death had blindsided her—Belinda was still alive, after all, just married to someone else—but he'd still felt raw and alone and frankly unlovable ever since she'd told him she wanted a divorce because there was someone else. The last thing he'd wanted ever since was to let another woman get close enough to him that she would rip his heart apart when the inevitable breakup happened.

Jeannie was different. She was making the reunion enjoyable, but he wanted more than just this one night.

He wanted to hold her in his arms. Sit with her while she snuggled next to him on his sofa so they could watch stupid movies or football games together—did she even like football?—and go out to dinner together and sleep in on Sunday mornings next to her after spending time with her the night before.

It seemed he wasn't gun shy after all. He'd just needed to find the right woman.

The right woman who lived in Arizona.

This would never work out. He couldn't move to Arizona. That was out of the question. Being as far away from Marri as he was, that was hard enough. He couldn't move farther away.

And Jeannie had her own business in Arizona. She'd already uprooted her life once before when she'd moved in with her daughter after her husband passed away. She'd been living in Sacramento at the time. He'd found that out when she said her parents had moved to Southern California.

"They like it far better than I liked Sacramento," she'd said. "Although Monterey was nice, but we didn't stay there for long."

She'd moved around, she'd said, because of her husband's job, but now it appeared she'd settled down in Arizona to be with her daughter. He could certainly understand that.

Even if she was on the same page he was, he couldn't ask her to move to Portland. She certainly appeared to be enjoying his company, but was she looking for a relationship?

Argh!

He felt like he was actually back in high school again himself, not merely attending a reunion. All these insecurities! He should be mature enough to talk these things out, but he knew it was far too soon.

He just needed to relax and enjoy himself tonight, and take whatever happened as fast or as slow as Jeannie wanted.

And if she wanted nothing at all beyond tonight?

Well, he could deal with that. He wouldn't want to,

but he had his daughter and a pretty damn good life. And he had the rest of the night.

He was determined to make this the best night she'd had in a long, long time.

CHRISTMAS REUNION

CHAPTER 13

Jeannie was having the time of her life.

She'd been flirting—yes, *flirting*—with Raymond for what seemed like hours. Marta and Lucas came and went. When all four of them were sitting around their table, they laughed and chatted and teased each other while the reunion went on around them.

And when Marta and Lucas left to go talk to someone else?

Then the conversation with Raymond got down to a more personal level. She'd told him she'd moved to Arizona the first part of the year, how wonderful it was to live with her daughter, and how she hadn't quite been prepared for the heat of an Arizona summer. She'd even talked to him about Jake, and for the first time in a long time, memories of Jake made her smile instead of want to cry.

She'd had a lovely life with Jake, and she didn't regret

a minute of it. Not when she found out she was pregnant long before they'd planned to have children, for how could she ever regret Kristen? Not when she'd been told that having another baby would be problematic because of Kristen's difficult birth. Not even when his job took them to Sacramento.

At first she'd felt guilty about having such a wonderful time with Raymond. She almost felt like she was betraying Jake, but her life with Jake was over. He wouldn't want her to spend the rest of her days with only his memory to keep her company. He'd want her to be happy.

And spending time with Raymond was definitely making her happy. She felt like a teenager again, only not the teenager she'd been in high school. She hadn't met Jake until after she'd graduated. Before then, her love life had consisted of a few sporadic dates and one disastrous junior prom.

Her prom date had been a gangly boy with an inflated opinion of himself. When it became clear to him that she wasn't going to "put out," as he'd called it, he ditched her to go out drinking with his buddies.

She'd been mortified.

Marta hadn't gone to their junior prom. School dances didn't fit with her ultra-disinterested-in-anything-remotely-mundane personality. The cheerleaders—especially Cissy—didn't even acknowledge Jeannie was alive back then, and she'd had no one to talk to after her date abandoned her.

She'd spent the rest of the night sitting by herself on

the bleachers, waiting for her date to come back. Eventually she'd called her parents to come pick her up.

She hadn't gone to her senior prom. One humiliating high school dance had been quite enough.

If only she'd known someone like Raymond back then, her junior prom would have been so much different.

No, wait—that wasn't quite right.

If she'd met Raymond back then, she wouldn't have married Jake, and she wouldn't have had Kristen. She wasn't exactly fatalistic about life—someone who believed that everything happened for a reason—but she believed her life had turned out the way it was supposed to. Except for Jake's passing, that is. They were supposed to have had at least another twenty or thirty years together.

This night made her wonder, though, if this was what high school life had been like for the popular girls. The ones like Cissy who'd always seemed to have a handsome boyfriend. Had they spent the evening flirting with the cutest boy in the room? Someone who made their hearts skip a beat like hers did every time Raymond looked at her as though she was the present he'd always wanted to find beneath his Christmas tree?

The four of them were sitting at the table now. Jeannie glanced over at Marta, who was looking like the happiest cat who'd ever eaten a fat canary. Or like a proud parent. It was a tossup.

Told you it would get better, Martha mouthed.

Jeannie felt her face heat up just a smidgen. It must

be pretty obvious that she was developing feelings for Raymond. Not that that was a bad thing. It might be a bad thing later, the proverbial morning after when reality reared its ugly head and plopped all the decisions she'd been putting off on her lap, but right now all she wanted was to enjoy the moment.

The background music switched to the opening few notes of "I'll be Home for Christmas."

Raymond leaned back in his chair and closed his eyes. "I love this song," he said.

"Is this the song I think it is?" Lucas asked.

Raymond cracked one eye open. "It might be," he said slowly.

Lucas chuckled. "I thought so. You have to do it."

Both of Raymond's eyes were open now as he mock-glared at his cousin. Clearly unabashed, Lucas only nodded toward Jeannie and grinned.

Raymond heaved out a sigh, but it was obvious he wasn't put out a single bit. "Okay, yes," he said as he leaned forward. "I have to do it." He stood up and turned toward Jeannie, holding out his hand. "Care to dance?"

Jeannie shot a *what's up?* glance at Marta.

"Don't look at me, girlfriend," Marta said. "I have no idea what they're talking about, and you know I don't like to dance."

At least she never used to, but the topic hadn't come up during any of their conversations. For all Jeannie knew, Marta went out clog-dancing on the weekends. Or maybe she'd learned the Charleston as one of her art school electives.

"Oh, come on," Lucas said to Marta. "Everyone dances to a song like this. Don't the words just pull at your heart?" He put a hand over his own heart as if to emphasize the point. "Life's too short not to be where you want to be at Christmas. I think life's too short not to have a little fun."

He stood up and pulled Marta to her feet.

"Okay, fine." She sounded more like an exasperated mom than a woman about to dance with the most flamboyant gay man in the room. "Between your suit and my outfit, we're going to be the most fabulous couple on the dance floor. But no groping, mister!"

"Trust me, my dear. You don't have the parts I'd want to grope."

And with that, off they went to go find the perfect spot on the dance floor where Lucas could show off.

That left Raymond still standing with his hand out, waiting for Jeannie to take it.

Well, what was she waiting for? This would be their first dance, and her heart sped up in anticipation.

She smiled and took his hand.

Jake had been a good dancer, but over the years, the times when they went out dancing together were few and far between. Work had always seemed to get in the way, and when they did go out of town on vacation, dancing wasn't on the agenda. Jeannie was afraid that she might be out of practice, but she needn't have worried.

Raymond turned out to be an amazing dancer.

Nothing fancy—no moves that made her worry about not stepping on his feet or tripping over her own. He put one hand on her waist and enfolded her other hand in his, tucking them against his shoulder.

They danced close enough to almost touch. "I'll be Home for Christmas" had a slow tempo, and she was relieved that most of what they did was sway to the melody. Having him so close was exhilarating and maddening at the same time. She wanted to be closer, to rest her head against his shoulder, close her eyes and lose herself in the moment.

But was it too soon for that? And should she make the first move? She had a feeling he'd been hurt deeply by his divorce. It wasn't so much what he'd said, but what he *hadn't* said. He'd talked lovingly about his daughter, a cute-as-a-button six-year-old. He hadn't mentioned his ex-wife except in a cursory way, and his eyes had tightened at the corners whenever he said her name.

Someone who'd been hurt that badly might not want to do anything more than flirt with her. What was the old saying? Once bitten, twice shy?

She tilted her head back to look up at his face, trying to gauge his emotions. Looking up at him like that didn't feel awkward. She tried to get a look at his expression. He seemed to be lost in thought even though every once in a while he squeezed her hand, almost like he was trying to reassure himself that she was still there.

After a moment, she said, "I've never danced to this song. What did Lucas mean when he said 'you just gotta'?"

"It's the lyrics," Raymond said. "About making a promise to be home for Christmas, all the while knowing you can't." His eyes got a far-away look. "My family always traveled to my grandparents' house for Christmas. From right after school got out until right before New Year's Eve, we were always gone."

She couldn't tell from his expression whether that was a cherished memory or something he'd merely put up with. When she was young, her family had never traveled anywhere for the holidays.

"It was fun when I was little," he said. "My grandparents spoiled me rotten. But once I hit high school and had a girlfriend? Not so much."

"You wanted to be with her at Christmas," Jeannie said. If she'd had a steady boyfriend during high school, she would have wanted to spend time with him during the holidays too.

"To be honest," he said, "I was hoping for a holiday kiss under the mistletoe. Which I see no one thought to include in these decorations." He arched a brow and gave her a wicked grin.

Her cheeks heated. Again. She hadn't blushed this much in one night since... well, since forever.

"Anyway," he said, "when I couldn't talk my parents into letting me stay home by myself, I made a tape. Of me singing this song for my girlfriend."

"You didn't!"

She and Marta had made mix tapes of their own favorite songs, but the thought of singing along with one of those songs had never occurred to Jeannie. She wasn't the world's greatest singer. Every now and then she'd sing a Christmas carol, always when she was by herself. She'd done a little better when she used to sing baby Kristen to sleep.

"I did," he said. "I wrapped it and put a big bow on it and gave it to her on the last day of school."

"Were you in chorus? Or choir?" Jeannie couldn't remember what the class had been called when she'd been in high school, but there had been some phenomenal singers at Parker High. Their performances had been the highlight of school assemblies.

"I was a football player," Raymond said. "And I can't carry a tune to save my life."

"Oh, no." Jeannie could just imagine what his rendition of the song must have sounded like. His voice wasn't as deep as someone like James Earl Jones, but it had a nice low resonance.

"Oh, yes," he said.

His grin softened, which made his face all that much more handsome.

This was a man who could look back at his teenage foibles with fond amusement. That said a lot about his character. He was clearly comfortable in his own skin or he wouldn't have agreed to be his gay cousin's plus-one for the night. That said even more.

The more she was learning about Raymond Ellis, the more she liked the person he seemed to be.

"I think she burned the tape after she listened to it," he said, "but it must have done the trick. After we got back home after Christmas, we... uh..."

Now he did look embarrassed.

"Are you sure you want to hear this part?" he asked.

He could tell her all about his silly teenage antics, but he was embarrassed to tell her he got lucky?

"I think I can fill in the blanks." She grinned up at him. "So now you feel compelled to dance every time you hear this song?"

"Dancing to this song led to the bank spot you just filled in." He moved her hand a little closer to his heart. "And no matter what Lucas thinks, I don't feel compelled to dance to it every time."

His thumb was stroking her hand ever so slightly. It sent little shivers up her spine. He was warm and tender and gentle, even though she could feel how solidly built he was beneath his suit.

"I only dance to this song when I have the right partner," he said.

Oh.

She did a mental blink.

Oh!

The nervous flutter she'd been feeling since she first touched his hand back when they'd introduced themselves to each other expanded to fill a spot in her heart she hadn't realized had been so empty. Jake had been her first real love, but that didn't mean she shouldn't live the rest of her life without ever falling in love again. Jake would want her to find a good man.

Was Raymond that good man?

Quite possibly.

Jeannie closed the distance between them so she

could rest her head against his shoulder. He wrapped his arm around her, and she leaned into him.

He felt incredibly warm and solid, and what's more, he felt *right*.

This was what she'd been missing in her life. This level of comfortable companionship which was very possibly leading to so much more. She'd been lonely, and she hadn't even known it.

As they danced to a song that had played a significant part of his teenage romantic life, she only had one wish.

That the song—and this dance—would never end.

CHAPTER 14

$\mathcal{J}$eannie felt incredible in Raymond's arms.

He'd surprised himself by telling her the story of how he'd attempted to woo Trish, the one high school girlfriend he'd been serious about, with the tape of him singing "I'll be Home for Christmas." Lucas, of course, knew all about it, but Raymond had never shared that story with Belinda. She would have made fun of him.

Jeannie hadn't teased him. Not one bit. In fact, he thought the story might have been the thing that finally made her relax and lean into him.

He'd wanted to enfold her in his arms the moment they hit the dance floor, but he hadn't wanted to push her. She'd maintained a discrete distance between them while they danced, and he understood. She was a recent widow. She probably had all sorts of rules she'd made for herself about what she could and couldn't do. Self-imposed barriers to any sort of intimacy with another man.

He'd been hurt enough by his divorce. He couldn't imagine the pain of losing someone he loved as much as she'd obviously loved her husband.

She was just the right height to fit comfortably in his embrace. It would be so easy to bend his head just a little and kiss her, but he told himself he'd have to take it slow. He'd have to let her decide when—or even if—they kissed.

They kept dancing, her head against his shoulder and his hand still enfolding hers, as "I'll be Home for Christmas" ended and another slow holiday song took its place.

He barely heard the music. The other couples dancing around them faded into the background until it seemed like the two of them were the only people in the whole world. The twinkle lights on the Christmas tree sparkled in the dim light of the gym, giving the night a magical feel. He knew he'd remember this dance for the rest of his life, and he found himself hoping that this was the first of many memories he'd make with Jeannie.

"I'm so glad I decided to come tonight," she said. "I almost didn't, this close to Christmas."

Raymond understood the feeling. He was going to have to give his cousin an extra special Christmas gift this year for making Raymond come to a reunion he didn't want to attend, not after he'd seen his suit. Jeannie hadn't made fun of him about his clothes either.

He decided to take a chance.

"You know," he said, "being here with you tonight,

it's something I didn't expect. And I've got to say, it's the best Christmas present I've had in a long, long time."

He almost held his breath, waiting to see how she'd react.

He felt her move closer to him, snuggle in against him. "I know exactly how you feel," she said.

They stayed dancing like that through the next two songs. They only moved apart when "Run, Run Rudolph" upped the tempo.

"Can't slow dance to that," he said, smiling down at her.

This close, he could see the fine lines at the corners of her eyes and smile lines around her mouth. Her eyes were glittering as she looked into his, and he knew—absolutely *knew*—she was the most beautiful woman in the world.

Oh yes, he was definitely in trouble. In the course of only a few hours—and a few magical dances—he'd fallen deeply in love.

"Let's go sit down for a while," she said. "I'm a terrible dancer with the faster stuff."

He doubted that, but sitting down sounded like a good idea.

It turned into an even better idea when she took his hand as they made their way back to their table.

Marta was sitting by herself. She looked happy—and tired.

"Jet lag," she said when Jeannie shot her a questioning glance. "And to think I get to do it all over again tomorrow."

"Are you sure you can't stay?" Jeannie asked.

Marta shook her head. "I can't even go to the brunch in the morning. My flight leaves at eight, which means I have to get to the airport at the crack of dawn to get through security." She looked at Raymond. "You wouldn't want to be Marta Gilroy for a day, would you?"

What?

"I have no clue what you mean," he said. He'd already (briefly) impersonated a gay man when he'd come through the balloon trellis with Lucas. He wasn't about to dress up as Marta, no matter what.

"You could take my place at the brunch," Marta said. "Unless you're going with Lucas?"

Lucas hadn't said a thing about going to the brunch. "Our deal was only for tonight," Raymond said.

"So that's perfect," Marta said. "You can go in my place, since I don't have a plus one and neither does Jeannie, I'm guessing. That way you two can hang out a little more together. If she's going." Her sleepy gaze shifted to Jeannie. "Are you?"

"I hadn't made up my mind," Jeannie said. "To be honest, once I decided to come tonight, I was waiting to see if I had a good time. If I didn't?" She shrugged one shoulder. "I'd know going to the brunch by myself would just be more torture."

"So..." Marta said. "You're going then? Because girl-friend, in case you haven't noticed, you're having a good time. And it's about time."

An adorable blush infused Jeannie's cheeks with just the right amount of pink. She let go of Raymond's hand and crossed her arms in front of her chest.

"You're incorrigible," Jeannie said to Marta.

"Never claimed to be anything else." Marta yawned widely then shook her head. "I think I need some coffee. Care to accompany me?" she asked Jeannie.

"You think the bar will have any?" Jeannie asked.

"Any good bartender should," Raymond said. The few times he'd been out late with friends from work, coffee had been everyone's last round. "Would you two care for some company?"

Marta shot him a look. "Someone has to hold our seats," she said. "You have no idea how valuable table seats are at this time in the festivities."

He was pretty sure she was putting him on, but as he looked around, he saw very few empty table seats. He was also pretty sure that Marta was using coffee as an excuse to get Jeannie alone.

"Okay," he said. "I'll just wait here for Lucas. Hold our seats. Like we're back in high school."

"Ha ha, very funny," Marta said, getting up. She stretched her back.

Jeannie got up too, although she looked like she didn't want to. "We won't be gone long," she said to Raymond. "Wait for me?"

He found himself grinning. "Always," he said.

And he meant it.

CHAPTER 15

The bar did, in fact, have coffee. Marta ordered three coffees, black.

Jimmy Jones, Chess Club President, was still working the bar. His Santa hat, as well as his Santa suit, looked a little worse for the wear. He'd apparently been very busy all evening, although there wasn't much of a crowd at the bar now.

There were still a few die-hard couples on the dance floor, but more and more people were sitting at tables or just standing around talking than the last time Jeannie had been at the bar. She'd been so wrapped up in her newfound feelings for a relative stranger that she hadn't noticed.

A relative stranger.

That thought brought her up short.

Raymond was a stranger.

Yes, they'd been talking for hours, and then they danced the way she wished she'd danced back when she'd gone to her one and only prom at Parker High, but he was still a stranger. She'd only met him a few hours ago. There'd been that zing of attraction when he'd shaken her hand, and the deeper attraction she'd felt when they were slow dancing together. He'd even admitted, in a way, that he had feelings for her.

But did he really mean it? Just because he was the cousin of Marta's friend Lucas, and just because he'd agreed to be a gay man's plus-one for the reunion and he had a daughter that he obviously adored, that didn't mean he wasn't playing on the emotions of a lonely widow.

Now that they were apart and she had time to think, she couldn't help but wonder why such a handsome, single man would be attracted to her. She was nothing special, just a pleasingly plump—okay, not so plump anymore—single woman in her forties who had absolutely no experience in the modern dating world.

In a way, he was no different than any of the other men who'd hit on her earlier in the evening. She'd only let him get close to her because of that initial bit of instant attraction and the fact that he was Marta's friend's cousin.

"You're talking yourself out of it, aren't you?" Marta asked.

She handed one of the coffees to Jeannie. It came in a holiday printed cardboard to-go cup, and the warmth seeping through the cup felt wonderful on her suddenly cold fingers. Now that she wasn't out on the dance floor—and leaning against Raymond—she realized that the gym was growing chilly. She must have acclimated to the heat of Arizona at least a little because now she was thankful for her sweater.

She blew on the coffee without answering Marta, and then took a careful sip. Surprisingly, the coffee was quite good. Strong enough without being too strong, with a great aroma and an even better flavor.

Technically, she didn't need the coffee. She wasn't jetlagged, and she'd only had one watered-down rum and Diet Coke and a very good Amaretto that Lucas had brought back for her. After that she'd stuck with sparkling water. Sipping at her coffee now was just a stalling tactic, like going for coffee had been Marta's way of getting her alone.

When it became clear Marta wasn't going to say anything else until Jeannie answered her question, Jeannie said, "I don't know what I'm doing. But I have been thinking that things are going along a little too fast."

Marta downed half her coffee before she came up for air. When they used to stop for early morning drinks at 7-Eleven all those years ago, Jeannie had always admired her friend's ability to drink a piping hot latte. If Jeannie had tried that, she would have scorched her throat.

"There," Marta said, coming up for air. "Now maybe I can stay awake long enough to talk some sense into you."

Jeannie raised an eyebrow. "Weren't you the one who's been telling me to be careful? Not to take drinks from strangers?"

That was actually a recent development. Something that Marta had teased her about when she'd not so subtly encouraged Jeannie to go out and enjoy life every once in a while, and maybe try dating again—when she was ready. Was she ready now? Raymond seemed lovely. In fact, he seemed just a little too good to be true.

If she actually lived in town, she could try dating him, see if the attraction she felt tonight was something that might turn into a lasting relationship. She could take it slow and discover if he was actually as good as he seemed. But she didn't live here. She wasn't even sure she wanted to move back to her old hometown. Seattle was a possibility, even if she didn't know anyone who lived there. She had good memories of her trip there with Jake but she wouldn't be running into things all the time that reminded her of all the happy years she'd spent being married to him, like she would if she moved back here.

"He's not exactly a stranger," Marta said. "Lucas says he's a good guy, if a little too tightly wrapped. That's coming from Lucas and his fabulously gay self, so take that part with a grain of salt. The tightly wrapped part, not the good guy part." She tilted her head to one side, and her voice softened. "Lucas says he hasn't dated much since his divorce."

"He actually said that?" Jeannie asked.

Marta glanced upward, as if trying to recall the exact conversation. "I think the way he put it was 'a monk living alone at the North Pole gets more action' than his cousin's had since his divorce. And probably for months before. Lucas doesn't think much of his cousin's ex."

That was certainly explicit. It also aptly described her dating life since Jake passed away.

"I still don't know him all that well," Jeannie said.

The reunion dance had turned into something of a Cinderella story. Jeannie wouldn't have to leave the ball at the stroke of midnight, but she would be leaving, not only the ball but the town. She'd already booked a flight back to Arizona to spend Christmas with Kristen and her boyfriend, something she was looking forward to.

"So go with him to the brunch," Marta said. "Spend some time with him before you fly away to cactus land. If you still have doubts?" She shrugged. "Then you have doubts. But don't write him off too quickly. Life's too short to miss out on something good."

That stung. "I know that," Jeannie said, a little more sharply than she intended.

Marta winced. "I'm sorry. I shouldn't have said it that way. You know that better than anyone. I'm tired and a little bitchy because I think you might be talking yourself out of something that could be the best thing that's happened to you in a while. And girlfriend, you deserve good things."

Marta's eyes were deep with honest emotion. She wasn't just saying things. She honestly believed the things she was telling Jeannie, even if she'd been thoughtless about how she'd said them.

Jeannie blinked the hurt away. "You didn't mean it like that, I know," she said. "I get that. I just..." She sighed. "This whole evening feels like it went off the rails. I didn't expect to meet anyone like Raymond tonight. I thought I'd be the only single person surrounded by a bunch of married couples—"

"Except me," Marta said.

"Yes, except you—and I didn't even think you were coming. But you know what I mean. I didn't expect to meet Mister—" She paused. She'd been about to say Mr. Right, but was he? "Incredibly Handsome and Incredibly Interested in *me*. I wasn't ready for this, you know?"

And was that part of the attraction? The need to feel like part of a couple because that's who'd she'd been for so long? Was that why she'd felt so good spending time with Raymond all evening?

"A lot of us aren't ready for the things that happen," Marta said. "And before you think I'm being thoughtless again, I didn't mean what's happened to you." She took another long swallow of her coffee. "Ever wonder why this is a Twenty-*Fourth* reunion that's being held in December, or all things?"

Jeannie had, and she admitted that.

"It's because of Cissy," Marta said. "When you hang around with Lucas all night, you hear a lot of gossip. Some of it's even accurate."

Cissy again. Only Marta's expression had turned serious. Jeannie felt a sudden clench of dread settle in her chest.

"What's going on?" she asked.

"She's sick," Marta said. "Looking forward to her twenty-fifth reunion next year was giving her something to focus on, but there's a chance now she might not be around next summer. So her friends threw this reunion together at the last minute just for her."

Jeannie was stunned.

This reunion was their Christmas gift to her.

So many things made sense now. Everything from the way Cissy had greeted her and all the hugs she'd gotten from women who hadn't given her the time of day in high school, to how thin Cissy was and why her hair was so short when she'd always worn it long in school, and why she'd hugged Jeannie so tight.

A hug that Jeannie hadn't returned.

Jeannie put her coffee down on the bar. "Watch this for me, Santa," she said to Jimmy.

She left Marta behind without another word. Marta would understand.

It was time to give Cissy a proper hug and wish her well.

Well past time, and life was too short to waste a minute of it.

CHAPTER 16

Marta came back to the table carrying two coffees, but without Jeannie.

Raymond raised a brow as she put one of the coffees down in front of him and plopped herself in one of the empty chairs. He'd been holding down the fort—or in this case the table—ever since Lucas ran off to talk to someone else he'd seen on the dance floor.

"I hope you like it black," she said. "It's actually not bad for bar coffee. Strong, but good."

Raymond was pretty sure he'd be up all night if he drank an entire cup of strong coffee at this late hour. He usually cut himself off around four in the afternoon. Marri had been a rise and shine at the crack of dawn toddler, and Belinda had always been a night owl. Raymond used to take the early shift with his daughter to give Belinda a little more time to sleep. Plus, it gave him extra daddy-daughter time before his workdays started.

He'd kept up the early-rising habit even after the divorce, which was fine because he was rarely out late at night. Although he'd happily stay awake until dawn tonight as long as he could spend that time with Jeannie.

Speaking of, he scanned the crowd looking for her, but he didn't see her.

"Did you lose your plus-one?" he asked Marta.

She leaned back in her chair, closed her eyes, and let out an audible groan. "I'm pretty sure she went to find Cissy." Marta slitted open one eye. "You know about that, right?"

"Know what about who?" He wasn't even sure who Cissy was.

"Blonde. About five foot nothing tall wearing a Santa hat. Former cheerleader who still has her figure."

He had a dim memory of having the stuffing hugged out of him at the check-in table by a total stranger who fit that description, but he couldn't remember the name printed on her nametag.

He gave her a shrug. "Still not really ringing any bells."

Marta gave her head a little shake. "Jetlagged. You have to forgive my poor memory. I'm usually much better than this. I keep forgetting you didn't go here. That you're a bit older than us. You wouldn't know our cheerleaders."

"Played some away games here," he said, "but that was it." While some of his buddies definitely noticed opposing teams' cheerleaders, he'd had his head totally in the game.

Marta sat forward and leaned her elbows on the table. "She was head cheerleader during junior and senior years, but I guess that was after your time. Unless you came back for away games after you graduated."

He shook his head no. He'd gotten a scholarship to the University of Oregon in Eugene. It was close enough to Portland that he could go home on a semi-regular basis, but not close enough to go back for a high school basketball or football game. Plus, he hadn't had much free time. He'd worked like crazy to keep his grades up so he wouldn't lose his scholarship.

"She probably hugged you and Lucas like crazy when you first got here." Marta sipped some of her coffee. "That's Cissy."

He'd been right. He'd thought she was pretty enough when he first saw her, but there'd been a brittleness about her too, like it wouldn't take much to break her.

"Is she one of Jeannie's friends?" he asked. Although she and Marta and Lucas had kept him entertained with stories about some of their classmates, Raymond had the impression she'd had few close friends during high school.

Marta gave a very unladylike snort. "Hardly, but Jeannie's got a soft heart."

"I noticed." It was just one more thing that made him fall for her. But he felt like he was coming in on the tail end of a conversation that had gone on without him. "I feel like I'm missing something here. You'll have to fill in the blanks."

She did.

In a very matter-of-fact way, Marta told him the story behind the reunion and Cissy's illness. "Jeannie knows what it's like to lose someone far too soon. That sometimes all you need is to know someone's there who cares."

Raymond stared down into his coffee.

That brittleness he'd noticed made sense now. He'd only met Cissy tonight, but he felt horrible for her. He wondered if she had any family. She certainly had the kind of friends who were more than simple acquaintances from school. They were family. They had done all this just for her, so that she had a chance to have the reunion she'd always wanted. That was a heck of a Christmas present.

He'd felt bad for himself after the divorce. He'd felt like his family had abandoned him. That the woman he'd loved had deserted him and taken his daughter from him. But they were still alive. He could still see them, see his daughter and be with her and do the kind of daddy-daughter things you could do with a six-year-old. He could still see her grow up. Saying goodbye to her whenever he dropped her off at Belinda's stung, but those goodbyes weren't permanent.

Not like the goodbye Jeannie hadn't been able to say to her husband.

"Did you know him?" Raymond asked. "Jake?"

Marta shook her head. "She met him after I went away to art school in New York City. We were still talking on the phone in those days. Not often, but we tried to keep in touch like we said we would. She told me about him, how she fell head over heels with him almost the moment she met him. I used to tease her about love at first sight. I told her she was living a cliché."

"That's what I told Lucas," Raymond said. "That he was living a cliché—the fabulously gay man. You know, he only wanted to come tonight to show off his fabulously gay, fabulously successful self."

"He's certainly been doing that." Marta grinned a tired grin. "But I understand the need to show off every now and then. I had an art teacher at that school in New York who told me I'd never amount to anything if I didn't shake up my style. I happen to like my style, and I told him so." She gave Raymond a sideways glance. "Politely."

He kind of doubted that, but he didn't say anything.

"Anyway," she said, "the first piece I sold that went for more than coffee money—*way* more than coffee money—I took that check and waved it in his face before I cashed it."

Raymond had thought about doing something like that with the first significant commission he'd earned. Only he'd wanted to wave it in front of his mother-in-law's face. Belinda's mother had always thought she'd married beneath her. That he'd never amount to anything.

He admired Marta for doing something he hadn't been able to do. Back then, he'd still been trying to keep the peace in his family.

"Cliché or not," Marta said, "Jeannie and Jake, they got married pretty soon after they met, then we both got busy..." She shrugged and sipped more of her coffee. "You know how it goes. You lose track, then forget that you lost track. Jake was one of the good guys, though. A rare find. The two of them were pretty much inseparable. You know, she was a great artist. Innovative in her own way. Back then, before we lost track, I kept trying to convince her to show some of her work—she does marvelous watercolors—but she never wanted to leave..."

She trailed off as her face went blank, and for a minute Raymond thought she might have dozed off in the middle of a sentence while still holding her coffee.

"Son of a—" Marta was looking off into the distance, but he could tell she wasn't looking at anything in the gym. "I'm an idiot."

He wasn't going to touch that line with a ten-foot pole.

"I bet that's the problem," Marta went on. "And if I didn't figure it out, I bet she hasn't either."

There was a problem? With Jeannie?

"You said problem," he said. "Is she all right?"

Marta didn't seem to hear. "She fell for Jake right away," she muttered. "Head over heels inseparable. Love at first sight. Then you come along, it's Jake all over..."

She glanced over at him, seemed to actually see him.

"Crap," she said. "I said that part out loud, didn't I."

He still felt like he was hearing only half of a conversation. It reminded him of the one-sided telephone conversations he had with his daughter from time to time.

"Enough to make me wonder what parts I missed," he said.

She sighed.

"You started this," he said. "If Jeannie has a problem, I'd like to help."

"Crap," she said again.

He waited. One thing being married had taught him was not to rush a woman who was trying to make a decision.

"Okay, here's the thing," she said finally. "We reconnected after her husband passed away. My mom might be a pain, but she's one of those women who keeps track of everyone. She's got a gossip chain you wouldn't believe. She's the one who told me about Jeannie's husband when he passed away. When Jeannie and I got on the phone together, it was like all those years we missed melted away. She told me *everything*, you understand?"

He nodded even though he didn't know where she was going with this.

"She was shattered," Marta said. "The kind of shattered that a lot of people don't come back from, but she's tougher than she thinks she is. I was always the brash one. I shoved my brash self in people's faces. Like me or not, nobody's going to ignore me because that's how I deal with potential rejection—get it over with and move on. Jeannie was always content to be in the background, that's how she figured she could keep herself safe, but she's tough underneath. She pulled through after Jake died. She did that by telling herself never again." She tapped the table with her index finger to drive her point home. "Never again. She wasn't going through that ever again. Then you come along." She gave him a long look. "*Now* do you understand?"

He sat back in his chair, stunned.

Of course. He'd been the idiot, not Marta.

He was falling for a widow, and she wasn't done grieving.

Grief changed people. The grief from his divorce had certainly changed him, although meeting Jeannie had gone lightyears into healing any residual hurt. Jeannie got through the worst of her grief by telling herself she'd never get close to another man again. It was a defense mechanism. It's how she dealt with the rest of the world.

"You're telling me she's been talking herself out of whatever's been happening between us tonight, aren't you," he said.

She shrugged. "Maybe. I dunno. It's late and I haven't been on this side of the country in decades. I'm probably not thinking straight. What I can tell you is that I've seen her happy tonight. Joyful. I haven't heard her like that *ever* in all the times we've talked on the phone since we reconnected." She downed the rest of her coffee. "I think what I'm telling you is to give her time. Let her set the pace. Can you do that?"

Could he? Right now he was willing to wait as long as it took.

"Yes," he said simply.

"Good." She pointed at his cooling coffee. "You going to drink that?"

He passed the coffee over to her. "You're going to be wired all night."

"I wish," she said. "Caffeine and I are old friends. We even occasionally sleep together." She took a long drink and sighed, then saluted him with the half-empty cup. "You're a good man, Raymond Ellis. I have a good feeling about you two."

He sincerely hoped she was right.

CHAPTER 17

Jeannie found Cissy sitting at the welcome table in the hallway outside the gym along with two other women Jeannie didn't know.

"Are you leaving us?" one of the women asked Jeannie. She was a pretty brunette with chubby cheeks and a pleasingly plump figure. Her nametag read *Maryellen Mayfield*. "Did you want your coat?"

Jeannie thought Maryellen might have been one of the cheerleaders who'd made the squad during their class's senior year, but she couldn't be sure. While she remembered Cissy, most of the other cheerleaders had faded into the background of her memory.

"No, not quite yet," she said. "I just wanted a moment with Cissy, if that's all right."

Cissy gave her a quizzical look, but she got to her feet. A little unsteadily, Jeannie thought.

"Cissy," the other woman—Lucy, according to her

nametag—said, her tone a gentle warning. "Don't overdo."

Cissy waved a dismissive hand at her. "I'll be fine, Mom." There was a warning buried behind her teasing tone. It sounded like Lucy might have been hovering a little too much, and Cissy'd had enough.

The door to the gym opened and a couple came out into the hallway trailing crowd noise and a few strains of the Carpenters' "Merry Christmas Darling" behind them. They were leaning on each other and grinning boozy smiles.

Jeannie caught sight of the nametag stuck to the man's sportscoat: *R. A. "Scooter" McClennon*. Their resident class clown, although his nametag didn't say that. Scooter had gained about fifty pounds in the last twenty-four years and had lost most of his hair, but he still had a sense of humor if his novelty tie was any indication. Not only was a red-nosed reindeer driving a sleigh pulled by tiny Santas across the navy blue silk of the tie, the reindeer's little red nose was a blinking light positioned right about where a tie tack would be.

Scooter and his date stumbled a few steps further into the hallway. They were definitely feeling no pain.

Cissy turned toward the women at the table. "We might want to call a car service for them, don't you think?"

The pretty brunette, Maryellen, got up from the table and went over to the extremely happy couple. "Hey, Scooter. Want to show me your keys? I bet you have a wildly inappropriate keychain."

Sure enough, Scooter fished his keys from his pants pocket and handed them over while the other woman at the table—Lucy—got out her cell phone.

Jeannie had to shake her head. She wondered if Maryellen worked at a bar or if she was just that good at getting people to do what she wanted. Jeannie made a mental note never to get on Maryellen's bad side. Not that she'd probably ever see her again.

A line from the Carpenters' song was playing on repeat over and over again in Jeannie's brain. Songs didn't usually do that, but this song, all about wishing to be together with the one you loved at Christmas, had been one of Jake's favorites. "That will never be us," he'd told her. "You'll never be alone at Christmas."

It had been a foolish promise made when their love was new and both of them thought they'd live forever.

That line made her think of another song about people in love being separated for the holidays. About how Raymond had recorded his version of "I'll be Home for Christmas" and sung it for his girlfriend. Jake would have never have thought of doing something like that, but he'd still been a very romantic man, especially around the holidays.

When Kristen was little, he'd wait until she'd gone to bed on Christmas Eve, then he'd turn out all the lights in the house except the lights on the Christmas tree. Mood lighting, he'd called it.

The two of them would snuggle next to each other on the sofa. Jake would put his arm around her shoulders and draw her in tight, and while they were sitting and enjoying the lights, he'd pull a gift out of his shirt pocket.

The gifts were sometimes silly—a gift certificate for two to a painting class where wine was served along with paper palettes of acrylic paint (as if she needed a class to know how to paint the picture everyone was supposed to be doing) or tickets to a community theater play—and sometimes serious, like the year he'd given her a necklace with three gold charms embedded with the birthstones for both of them and for their daughter.

She still had that necklace in her jewelry box. She hadn't been able to bring herself to wear it since he'd passed away.

She would miss sitting next to him on Christmas Eve, just enjoying the lights on the tree. Would miss the comfortable familiarity of his arm around her shoulder. Would miss the anticipation of wondering what gift he'd have for her this year in his shirt pocket, but most of all she'd just miss *him*.

Jeannie gave herself a mental shake. She hadn't gone looking for Cissy because she was feeling sorry for herself.

Cissy glanced at Jeannie's nametag. "Jeannie Carlson," she said. "That's right. I remember you from earlier. Were we friends in school? My memory's not what it used to be."

"I was Jeannie Bishop back then," Jeannie said. "We weren't friends. I hung around with Marta Gilroy. Goth girl, long black hair. Always dressed in black."

Cissy took a moment, then she grinned and nodded.

"I remember you now. The two of you were always together. Artists, right?"

That surprised Jeannie so much she almost didn't answer. She always thought she'd been invisible to the popular girls.

"Marta is," she said. "She has gallery shows of her art all the time. I'm—"

What? A graphic designer? A mom?

A widow?

"Not," she finished lamely.

Cissy gave her a quizzical look, as if she was looking for the hidden meaning behind the pause. "You know," she said, "I always envied you two just a little."

Cissy envied *her?* "Why on earth would you?" Jeannie blurted out, but Cissy didn't seem to take offense.

"Because you were so different," Cissy said. "And you didn't care that you were different. In fact, your friend— Marta?—she wore it like a badge of honor."

Jeannie shook her head. "Marta could do that. I just followed her lead."

"Well, it worked for you." Cissy shrugged. "I went the other way. Wear the right clothes, date the right person. Get married and have two point five children. Well, I didn't get that last part right," she said, almost like an afterthought.

Jeannie wondered if she meant the children or the marriage. Cissy wasn't wearing a wedding ring.

"Do you have children?" Cissy asked.

"One daughter," Jeannie said. "She's in graduate school."

Cissy blinked, clearly having done the math. "Wow, that's wonderful. Congratulations. And your husband?"

Jeannie just shook her head.

"Me either." Cissy wiggled the fingers on her ringless left hand. "I married the quarterback, but he didn't stick around for the long haul." She shrugged. "He wanted kids, and I... well, that wasn't in the cards."

Jeannie didn't know what to say to that. Cissy hadn't mentioned her illness, and Jeannie didn't think she should bring it up. She especially didn't want Cissy to think that Jeannie was only talking to her because she was feeling sorry for her.

That thought brought her up short.

Why *had* she felt compelled to see Cissy again? To discuss grief with a dying woman? That was all kinds of wrong.

Jeannie began to think that she'd made a mistake tracking Cissy down. She'd had some sort of impulse to tell Cissy how sorry she was about Cissy's situation, but this wasn't a woman who'd accept that kind of sentiment. Cissy was still clearly in charge of her own life, and she wouldn't take well to pity of any kind.

Jeannie should have known that. She'd hated how people had treated her after Jake died, like she was made of glass that might shatter at any moment. Or they'd tell her how sorry they were for her loss, like they were just waiting for her to break down in front of them. Grief vultures with greedy eyes and barely concealed glee at someone else's misery. The last thing Jeannie had wanted was the pity of relative strangers.

Cissy interrupted Jeannie's thoughts with a smile that didn't quite reach her eyes. "You know, I saw you out on the dance floor," she said. "Your dance partner looked like a keeper. He wasn't in our class, was he? I think I would have remembered him."

Jeannie felt her cheeks flush. "No. He's a few years older than we are."

"Lucky woman," Cissy said. "Tall, dark, and handsome, and crazy enough to wear a suit like that."

Lucky woman? Jeannie realized Cissy thought Raymond was her partner for more than just a dance.

"Oh, no," she said. "We're not together. I just met him tonight."

Understanding dawned in Cissy's eyes. This time her smile looked entirely genuine. "I repeat. Lucky woman. Because from what I saw, that man is totally into you."

And that was the problem, wasn't it. That was the thing that threw cold water onto the happiness she'd felt dancing with him. With his strong hand enfolding hers and holding it against his chest. She'd felt happy and safe and more than a little attracted to him, and more than just the way that single zing she'd felt when their hands touched for the first time made her feel.

Raymond was totally into Jeannie, and she was... what? Flattered? Infatuated? Falling for him?

She'd fallen in love before at first sight. With Jake.

The first time she'd seen him—in a department store, of all things—she'd thought he was the handsomest man she'd ever met. She'd been in the stationery aisle, stocking up on pens, mechanical pencils, and notebooks for her first semester in community college. He was looking for supplies for work. He'd just been promoted, and he had a week-long training seminar where he expected to take copious notes. He had a certain type of pen he preferred, which he hoped would help stave off getting any cramps in his hand.

They'd bumped into each other while Jeannie was trying to decide between gel pens and regular ink pens. She'd never used gel pens before, but she was intrigued by the variety of colors and point sizes. They'd both reached for the same pack of pens at the same time, and their fingers had brushed up against each other.

Before tonight, that had been the only time Jeannie had ever felt a zing of instant attraction. But with Jake it had been more than just that. When she'd looked into Jake's startled eyes—he'd told her much later that he'd felt the same zing—she'd felt a strong, immediate connection. Like a thread that had always existed between them had suddenly been pulled tight.

She told him much later that it had felt like the universe had given her a kick in the shins that had set off delightful shivers throughout her body and warmed her heart.

Love at first sight.

It didn't feel like that with Raymond. Close, but not quite the same thing. With Raymond, the zing she'd felt when they'd touched hands had been more like a comfortable kind of homecoming. Like he was the exact right person to fill the place in her heart that had been empty for months.

"I don't really know him," she told Cissy.

"But isn't that part of the fun?" Cissy asked. "Getting to know each other? You don't always have to be friends first. Sometimes you just get hit with a clue-by-four between the eyes, and realize that yes, this is the one."

Jeannie'd already had The One. No one could compete with Jake.

But if she truly believed no one could ever compete with what she'd already had—and lost—that meant she'd be living the rest of her life without love. That looked like a pretty bleak future.

Cissy's smile faded, and Jeannie could see a pinched look at the corner of her eyes. She was hurting, and she looked—for just a moment—like she was beyond tired. Maybe Lucy had been right. Cissy was overdoing it.

Cissy bit at her lower lip, then lowered her gaze. "I'm probably butting in where I shouldn't, but if you can't hand out unwanted advice at Christmas, when can you?" She looked up at Jeannie, her expression suddenly serious. "I can see you hesitating. Weighing the odds. Maybe making a few unfavorable comparisons? I don't know what happened to your marriage, that's your business. But life doesn't always give us second chances. Enjoy them while you can."

There was an undertone of melancholy behind the words. According to what Marta had said, Cissy had been focusing on the reunion as a way of coping with what was coming at her in the next few months. Now that the reunion was just about over, what would she focus on now? Jeannie hoped Cissy's friends had something else in mind for her to enjoy. While she still could.

"I'll think about it," Jeannie said. "I promise."

"Don't think about it. Just enjoy it while you can."

They shared a look. Jeannie saw a lot of pain in Cissy's eyes. She didn't know what Cissy saw in hers, but she glanced away quickly, then cleared her throat. "I get the feeling all this wasn't what you wanted to talk to me about," Cissy said.

The moment was over. Jeannie gave herself a mental shake.

"I wanted to give you a proper hug," she said. "You surprised me the first time around and I just stood there."

Cissy shook her head. "You and Marta. You were always the most unique people in our graduating class."

Jeannie cut a look toward Scooter. "We did have a few other people who were really unique."

"Special, I believe, was the term we used." Cissy held her arms open wide. "Come give me a proper hug, Jeannie Bishop Carlson. Just don't squeeze too hard. My ribs can't take it like they used to."

So Jeannie did. She wrapped her arms around Cissy and held her—not too tight—for a long moment. Cissy smelled like cinnamon and vanilla, but it didn't quite mask the underlying medicinal scent. Her shoulder blades were prominent beneath Jeannie's hands, and

Jeannie realized Cissy's sexy red dress had been designed to hide exactly how thin she'd become.

"You know," Cissy said as she patted Jeannie's back, "you can always give this guy a try. If it doesn't work out? Call it quits. Regrets are for the things we pass up because we're too scared to try, and life's too short to accumulate a bunch of those things."

Life *was* too short. Jeannie hadn't forgotten that, she'd just refused to think about it in terms of her own life. While she hadn't exactly wasted the months since she'd moved in with her daughter—grieving was a natural process she had to go through, and everyone processed grief differently—she hadn't really done much of anything else that she didn't have to. She'd filled the hours with work and books and just sitting in the sunroom. Almost like she was in a holding pattern, waiting for something to happen.

Was Raymond that something?

Yes, he was a stranger, but every new person in her life had started out as a stranger. Even Jake had been a stranger when she'd first met him in the stationery aisle.

What was she so scared of? That she might actually develop real, deep feelings for another man? That wouldn't mean she'd loved Jake any less. Her love for Jake would always be there, more than a simple memory, but no longer living and vibrant.

And there was one more question, maybe the most important one:

Would she regret it if she blew Raymond off without getting to know him better?

The answer to that was yes.

She'd felt so comfortable with him all evening. She didn't really want this night to end, and that alone should tell her something.

She and Jake had planned to retire in their old hometown. Could she really do that on her own? Restart her life by going back to the beginning? The town had changed. Of course, it had, but she'd changed too. Nothing in life ever stayed the same. Not holiday traditions. Not the people in your life. Not even an old 7-Eleven, and were there even any Dairy Queens still left?

Her closest friend from her teenage years had moved to New York. If she moved back here, she really would be starting over. Starting from scratch. Making new friends.

Like Lucas.

Like Raymond.

Would getting to know him better be the right decision? Was he actually as good as he seemed? As much as her heart insisted he was?

She needed time to find out. Tonight had been a good start. But it wasn't over yet.

By the time she let go of Cissy, Jeannie had made at least one decision.

"About tomorrow's brunch," she said. "Can I bring a plus one?"

CHAPTER 18

Raymond was still saving the table—along with a very sleepy Marta—when Lucas returned from his latest round of show-offs. Only this time he wasn't alone.

Lucas introduced the man with him as Orlando Gamboa. Orlando had been a wrestler in high school. He'd had no classes with Lucas and pretty much hadn't known Lucas existed. Lucas hadn't known Orlando either, otherwise he might have known he wasn't the only gay student at Everett Parker High.

Orlando. Of course Lucas would find a good-looking gay man at the reunion who just happened to be named *Orlando*.

"Pleased to meet you. Orlando," Raymond said, putting a little too much emphasis on the man's name.

"Oh, hush," Lucas said. "I told him all about my Legolas fixation."

Orlando glanced at Lucas with an indulgent smile.

He might have had the body of a wrestler in high school, but he was a slender man now, with deep brown eyes, dark brown hair, and just enough muscles beneath a tight Christmas sweater to hint at his athletic past.

"He's not the only one who had a crush on a certain elf," Orlando said. "I liked the actor too, but it was weird to say I liked another guy named Orlando, so I told everyone it was the pointy ears that did it for me."

That led into a lively discussion between Lucas and Orlando about the Rings movies and who—besides a pointy-eared elf—was the hottest actor among the cast. Both of them had bottles of sparkling water, and they occasionally clinked the bottles together when they agreed on a point. Marta stuck with Raymond's coffee.

When the minutes stretched out and Jeannie still hadn't come back, the one thing that gave Raymond hope that he'd see her again was the fact that she hadn't said goodbye to Marta. He didn't think she was the kind of woman to just ditch her best friend.

Raymond was about ready to go find her, to make sure she was okay, when he saw her walk through the balloon trellis at the entrance to the gym.

The sight of her still took his breath away. She looked as amazing as she had the first time he'd seen her. The lavender sweater set off her dark hair and soft blue eyes, and the dark blue slacks made her legs look long and slender. She carried herself with a self-confidence that wasn't just an act. She was comfortable in her skin, and she made his heart beat faster just looking at her.

"Close your mouth, big boy," Lucas said. "Or at least

if you're going to drool over a woman you just met, you should attempt to be cool about it."

Raymond shot him a look. "Give me a break. I'm out of practice."

Lucas rolled his eyes. "Lord, don't I know it."

"I think I'm missing something," Orlando said.

"You're missing a lot," Marta said around a yawn. She got up and held out a hand to Orlando. "Come with me and I'll fill you in."

Orlando got up from the table with a definite swish of his hips. "And where are you taking me?"

"To get more coffee for me and more sparkling water for the cousins and my best bud from high school. You'll get to meet Jeannie in a minute."

"Can't wait," Orlando said with a grin as the two of them headed for the bar.

"Don't dawdle," Lucas called after them.

"You're insufferable," Raymond said to his cousin. "You're giving me a hard time, and here it took you all night to latch on to the only other gay man in the place."

"Who says he's the only other gay man?"

Raymond chuckled. It figured. All that going off to talk to people Lucas hadn't seen in nearly a quarter of a century. He hadn't been just talking up his successful clothing line. He'd been scoping out possible dating material.

When Raymond didn't take the bait, Lucas said, "Santa number two, in case you're wondering. The other gay man? He's delightful in his own swarthy way, but his name isn't Orlando." He sighed a contented sigh as he watched Marta lead Orlando to the bar. "It's destiny, don't you think?"

"Well, there's one sure way to tell," Raymond said. He paused, drawing out the suspense, until Lucas cocked an eyebrow. "Does he like your clothes?"

Lucas batted his eyelashes behind his burgundy-framed glasses. "Silly boy, he likes the whole package." He gestured with his head toward where Jeannie was only a few tables away now and still headed in their direction. "I think she likes your whole package too, which is my cue to go see what trouble Ms. Marta is getting into with my very own sexy elf."

He got up from the table and gave Jeannie a little finger wave, then he was gone.

Leaving Raymond sitting all alone, waiting for her and hoping she wasn't coming to tell him she'd had a lovely evening but she really must be going.

Much to his relief, she wasn't.

Instead of sitting down, she held her hand out to him. "Care to dance?" she asked.

She had a mischievous grin on her face, and he could swear she had a sparkle in her eyes.

"That's the best offer I've had all night," he said, smiling back.

The music had switched over to almost all slow, soulful holiday music. As they took to the dance floor, Nat King Cole was singing about chestnuts roasting on an open fire. Raymond took Jeannie in his arms and she laid her head on his shoulder, her arms wrapped around his waist.

"Thanks for waiting for me," she said. "I went to go see Cissy."

"That's where Marta thought you might have gone." He paused for a beat. "She said Cissy's health isn't good."

After losing her husband not that long ago, it must have taken a lot for Jeannie to go see someone else with a terminal illness. Raymond admired the courage it took to do something like that. Would he have been as brave? He liked to think so, but he'd never been put to the test.

Jeannie nodded against his chest. "We didn't talk about that, but it was clear she's not feeling well. Her friends put this entire reunion on just so that she could enjoy it while she's still up to enjoying it. They're very protective. Although I wouldn't be surprised if she outlives their expectations. She's a pretty strong-willed woman."

"She's not the only one," Raymond said.

"You mean me?" She shook her head. "I'm not strong-willed. If I was, it wouldn't have taken me so long to…" She trailed off with a sigh.

He felt her tense up just the slightest. He took a chance and placed a soft kiss on the top of her head. "Don't be so hard on yourself," he said. "It must have taken a lot for you to decide to come here tonight."

He hadn't wanted to go anywhere right after his divorce. The few times he'd agreed to meet someone, usually a friend of someone at work, the whole thing had been worse than a trip to the dentist. He'd felt bad for the women afterwards and decided he'd be better off alone until the time was right. He hadn't thought the right time was right now, but apparently the universe had other ideas.

He admired Jeannie's inner strength for coming to the reunion by herself. For walking through that balloon trellis alone when she'd been part of a couple who'd clearly adored each other for over twenty years.

She took a deep breath, almost like she was steeling herself for something. His heart felt tight, and he hoped he hadn't blown things with that little kiss. He'd meant it only as a comfort, but now he hoped he hadn't reminded her of how much she missed her late husband because he used to kiss the top of her head too.

"I'm glad I did decide to come," she finally said, a slight tremor in her voice. "Otherwise I wouldn't have met you."

She tilted her head up like she was trying to read his reaction. When he glanced down into her upturned face, the expression there took his breath away. She was truly the most beautiful woman he'd ever seen, hands down, and she was looking at him like he was the only man in the world she wanted to be with.

He almost kissed her then—he wanted to kiss her, really kiss her, her more than anything he'd ever wanted in his life—but he told himself he needed to wait for her to make the first move.

Had that been it? The move?

Did she want him to make the first move?

Was she waiting for him?

The reunion must have regressed his mind right back to high school. All this indecision! He was a grown man with a daughter of his own. He should be able to decide whether a woman wanted a kiss. He was so out of practice, it wasn't even funny.

She moved one hand away from his waist and fumbled something from the pocket of her slacks, then held it over their heads. Or as close to over their heads as she could get.

"Look what I found," she said. "Someone left it lying on the front table, can you imagine that?"

It was a plastic sprig of mistletoe.

"It's not 'I'll be Home for Christmas,'" she said, "but it was the best I could do on short notice."

That was the move he'd been waiting for. No mistaking it for anything else.

He grinned at her, then bent his head to kiss her.

Right there in the middle of a high school gym at a reunion for a school he'd never gone to, at a dance he hadn't wanted to attend.

He kissed this woman who'd clearly captured his heart.

He kissed her tenderly, not wanting to press her. Her lips felt amazingly soft against his, and something in his chest loosened. All the years of being alone, of locking up his feelings and pretending that it didn't matter that his ex had stopped loving him long before she'd divorced him. Of pretending that he didn't care that the divorce left him feeling like he'd never find love again because he didn't deserve it, hadn't deserved it the first time—all of it melted away in that one first gentle kiss.

It could have gone on forever and he would have been a happy man.

Of course, it couldn't, but that didn't matter.

Because when he looked in Jeannie's eyes this time, her happy gaze held the promise of many more kisses yet to come.

CHAPTER 19

The kiss had been amazing. Far better than anything she could have imagined.

Jeannie had been so nervous she was shaking inside, unsure of whether she could actually go through with something as corny as holding a sprig of mistletoe over their heads while they danced. But she'd had a feeling when they'd first gone out on the dance floor that he'd been waiting for her to send him a sign, some sort of signal, before he would kiss.

She wasn't self-confident enough to just reach up and kiss him on her own. She hadn't kissed another man in over two decades, so a corny prop would have to do.

After all, he was a man who'd made a tape of him singing a Christmas carol for his girlfriend when he knew he couldn't carry a tune. She hoped he'd just go with the whole idea and not make her feel stupid.

She shouldn't have worried. The mistletoe did exactly what mistletoe had done for so many other people.

It gave them a reason to kiss.

His mouth on hers had felt so right, she wondered what in the world she'd been so worried about. He tasted vaguely of coffee, and his lips felt as tender as she'd imagined. There was no spark this time, no zing of electricity, but there was something better. Something that made her feel like she'd found a new home, a new place to belong—right in his arms—and she'd melted against him.

When the kiss ended, he looked at her with such tenderness in his eyes that her heart felt like the Grinch's, expanding and breaking through the icy cold aloneness that she'd been living with ever since Jake passed away.

"I don't think we need the mistletoe anymore," he said.

She giggled. She actually *giggled*. When was the last time she'd done that?

"No, we don't," she said. She tucked the sprig back in her pocket. She'd find another table to leave it on. Maybe another couple could put it to good use just like they had.

Another couple.

She'd actually thought that. That they were a couple. Premature, much? It had been a wonderful kiss, but it was still just one kiss. They had a lot of getting to know each other left to do.

Speaking of...

"Do you have plans tomorrow morning?" she asked.

He smiled at her. "What did you have in mind?"

"There's this champagne brunch I heard about," she

said. "It's supposed to be pretty good, according to Cissy."

A small line formed between his brows. "I don't have to pretend to be Marta, do I?"

She giggled again. Just the idea of him dressing like Marta was one of the funniest things she'd heard in a while. He might actually do it. He'd worn the shiny green suit Lucas had made for him after all.

"No," she said. "I told Cissy I'd be bringing a plus one."

"And she was okay with that?"

Okay with it? She'd practically beamed when Jeannie had asked her. Like a proud parent whose kid just did the hardest thing in the world. Jeannie had thought it would be hard to ask him to come to the brunch with her. It was almost like asking him out on a date, after all. But it had been so easy.

What had she been so worried about?

"Definitely," Jeannie said. "So will you come?"

He wrapped his arms around her and held her tight, then pressed a kiss on the top of her head again. Jake had never done that, but Jeannie liked it. It made her feel warm and loved and cared for.

"Try to keep me away," he said.

Christmas Eve in Portland was cold and rainy. Raymond had gotten up entirely too early, even for him. But he'd guessed—correctly—that the drive to and from Tacoma to pick up his daughter for Christmas would be a bear thanks to holiday traffic, and he'd wanted to get an early start.

He'd planned to keep Marri busy with her favorite games on her nearly indestructible tablet, a model made just for kids, but her mind hadn't been on her games.

It had been on Santa.

And that meant she hadn't settled down enough to doze off at all during the drive like she usually did. By the time they got to his house, she was tired and cranky and very, very concerned that Santa would be able to find her at Raymond's house.

"It's your house too, sweetie," he told her every time she'd asked. He'd even showed her the Christmas stocking with her name on it that he'd hung on his fireplace mantel.

Right next to the stocking with Jeannie's name on it.

Jeannie had stayed in town for an extra three days following the reunion. They'd spent nearly every minute together except for the times that Raymond simply couldn't get away from the office.

Somehow they'd never managed to talk about his job at the dance, but when he'd mentioned during the champagne brunch that he was a realtor, her eyes lit up.

It turned out that one of the reasons she'd decided to come to the reunion was to reacquaint herself with her old hometown. She and her husband had planned to move back to the area after he retired. She couldn't live with her daughter forever, and she thought she'd see if moving back—without Jake—was something she wanted to do.

"Kristen's got her own life," Jeannie had said. "It's time for me to move on."

Since she didn't get along with the climate in Arizona, the reunion gave her the opportunity to check out the housing situation around Portland.

Up until that point, Raymond had been deliberately ignoring the logistical aspects of their budding relationship. He figured that if the relationship was headed the way he hoped it was, they'd work something out. He was even willing to rack up a bunch of frequent flyer miles. He'd never been to Arizona, and who knew. He might like it.

Now it looked like he might not have to. *Might* not,

he kept reminding himself. She'd only just started to think about where she might like to live. She'd mentioned Seattle, but she'd also said she didn't know anyone there. She'd just liked the area the one time she'd been there.

Raymond could work with Seattle. It wasn't that far from Tacoma, and he was already making that trip on a regular basis.

He'd suggested that wherever she might like to live, she should consider a short-term lease. "Say six months," he'd said. "It would give you a chance to get your bearings. See if you really like the area without making a longer commitment."

She'd agreed that sounded like a good idea. They'd spent most of the three extra days she'd stayed in town looking at possible rentals. Not only rental houses in her old hometown, but also condos closer to the heart of Portland.

Closer to where he lived.

"If I decide to buy something," she'd said, "I'd rather have a house, not a condo. But for the short term, a condo would be fine." She'd grinned at him. "No yard work."

His own yard was somewhat neglected, something he'd joked about the first time they'd had an early takeout dinner at his house. "I've kind of let it go," he'd admitted.

He'd also neglected the inside of his house. It was neat and clean, but the furnishings were definitely on the sparse side. Even the Christmas decorations he'd put out —the tree with all the old ornaments Belinda hadn't wanted and the lights and the few strands of garland he'd hung around the fireplace—seemed sparse now that he looked at them the way he thought Jeannie might see them.

"Looks like a bachelor pad, doesn't it?" he'd said.

She'd shrugged. "It looks like you're a man whose job keeps him busy."

He was pretty sure she was just being nice, and then he'd asked her if she had any suggestions how to make it homier, especially for his daughter for Christmas since she was getting to the age when she noticed things.

Jeannie did.

Then the two of them had gone shopping.

He'd never had so much fun shopping in his life. He'd taken Jeannie to all his favorite stores, then he'd taken her to all of Lucas's favorite stores, including a year-round Christmas boutique that looked like Santa's workshop had exploded inside a renovated two-story house.

It might seem silly, but he felt like Jeannie's touch had turned his house into something special. She'd added potted poinsettias on each side of the fireplace hearth after he'd told her that he had no pets and rarely used the fireplace for an actual fire. They'd replaced the logs he'd left in the fireplace but never lit with real pine branches, and then arranged candles among the boughs. The candles had little flickering electric flames instead of real ones—no fire hazard, she'd said—and for a final touch, nestled scented pinecones on the branches.

They'd added a few new Christmas ornaments to the

tree. The new ornaments featured his daughter's favorite cartoon characters. Then they'd hung a new stocking from his mantel, a quilted stocking with his daughter's name embroidered on the cuff.

The whole thing made his house not only feel but also smell like Christmas. "Top it off with hot chocolate and Christmas cookies for Santa," Jeannie had said, "and you'll be a hit with your daughter."

Before he'd left to go pick up his daughter, he'd put a few presents for her under the tree. He'd add more after she went to bed—presents from Santa all wrapped in special paper featuring vintage Santas that Jeannie had helped him pick out at the Christmas boutique. He'd also put a few small things in her stocking wrapped in the same paper.

"Santa always uses his own wrapping paper," Jeannie had said.

The decorations had been a hit with Marri—or as much of a hit as they could be to an overtired six-year-old on Christmas Eve. She'd been more interested in the presents under the tree, but he'd told her she'd have to wait until the morning to open them.

He'd selected a Christmas music channel on one of his streaming services, and over hot chocolate and chicken pot pie—her favorite—they'd sat in the living room on the sofa that was now positioned to face the tree while Marri chatted happily about her visit with Santa after Thanksgiving and everything she'd asked for in the letter to Santa her mom had helped her write.

Raymond was thankful that at least a few of the

things she'd told Santa about were now wrapped in the Santa wrapping paper and hidden away in his closet.

There was one other present wrapped carefully and put away in his closet. This one wasn't wrapped in the special Santa paper, and it didn't have Marri's name on it. This one was for Jeannie, and he planned to put it in her stocking after Marri went to bed.

After Jeannie had left to return to Arizona, he'd gone to the same store where they'd found Marri's stocking. He'd purchased one for Jeannie, which he hung in between Marri's stocking and the simple felt stocking Jeannie had purchased for him. His stocking already had a present stuffed inside. He planned to leave her stocking hanging on the mantel until she came back to town.

She hadn't firmed up the date yet, but she'd be coming back to Portland toward the end of January. This time she'd be staying with him while she finalized the lease on a condo not too far from the café with the Middle Earth theme. They'd had coffee there after she'd viewed the condo, and she'd said it was the café as much as the condo itself that made her decide that was the place for her.

It seemed she had a crush on Aragorn. Raymond could live with that.

They were still in the early stages of their relationship, but he had a good feeling about the two of them. That's why he'd bought her the charm bracelet that he'd wrapped and put in her stocking. Maybe it was old fashioned, and it was probably meant more for a teenager than someone their age, but it had seemed perfect considering how they'd met at a high school reunion.

He'd added two charms to the bracelet—a sprig of mistletoe and a music note.

With any luck, he'd be able to add two more charms next Christmas, and two more the Christmas after that. And when the bracelet got too full, he'd buy her a second one.

That's what you did when you were in love, and he most definitely was.

And he was most definitely tired.

"Don't you think it's about time you went to bed?" he asked his daughter after she yawned for what had to be the tenth time.

"Not tired," she mumbled around another yawn.

She already had on her Christmas pajamas, and she'd been snuggling under a Christmas plaid fleece blanket—another addition to his house thanks to Jeannie—for the last half hour.

"Well, I'm tired," Raymond said. "If we both go to bed early, Santa will have plenty of time to get here and leave you presents."

"In my stocking?" Marri asked.

"In your stocking," he said, "and maybe some under the tree. You won't know until tomorrow morning."

Just like he wouldn't know until tomorrow morning what Jeannie had slipped in his stocking. "Don't open it early," she'd said.

Leaving it alone had been killing him with curiosity,

but he'd waited with almost as much anticipation as Marri had about Santa's visit.

"I should stay up and thank Santa," Marri said. "Mommy says it's polite to say thank you."

"That it is," Raymond said. "But I think Santa already knows when kids thank him. Kids don't have to tell him in person. It's in the contract."

Marri frowned at him. "What's a contract?"

"Something you'll learn about when you get a little older." He stood up and then picked up his daughter, fleece blanket and all. "Right now it's off to bed with you."

She gave him a curious, sleepy look as he carried her to her bedroom. "You look happy, Daddy. Are you happy?"

He didn't even have to think twice about that answer. He gave his daughter a hug and a kiss on the cheek. "Yes, sweetie. Daddy's happy. How about you?"

She gave him a solemn nod. "Yes," she said. Then she yawned again and snuggled in against him.

She was asleep by the time he put her in her bed and pulled up the covers.

He stood watching her sleep for a few long moments. He had his daughter with him on Christmas Eve and the start of a new relationship with a beautiful woman he hoped would be in his life for the rest of his life. Oh yes, he was happy. He was happier now than he'd been in years.

This was going to be a very Merry Christmas after all.

CHAPTER 21

Christmas morning was clear and relatively cool —at least by Arizona standards.

Jeannie sat with her usual cup of coffee in the sun room. Kristen and her boyfriend Michael were in the kitchen making brunch. Jeannie would have offered to help, but they needed some time on Christmas morning to be by themselves. They were making their own Christmas memories, just the two of them, and Jeannie was more than happy to give them the space they needed to do that.

Michael had proposed to Kristen the night before, and she'd said yes. Jeannie had never seen her daughter so happy before. They'd made Brandy Alexanders to celebrate, something Jeannie's parents used to drink on Christmas Eve, and watched *Love Actually* while Kristen and Michael sat on the sofa, their arms around each other.

Then he'd slept over.

Yes, it was definitely time for Jeannie to move into a place of her own.

She snuggled back against the comfortable contours of the barrel chair and gazed at the flowers that had arrived that morning. Red roses and white carnations with sprigs of pine and holly and tied with a red plaid bow. The vase was covered with holiday-patterned fabric, and a plush red-nosed reindeer peeked over the back of the arrangement.

The card accompanying the flowers had read *Merry Christmas, beautiful. Raymond.*

The flowers and the card warmed her more than any cup of coffee ever could.

She'd wanted to call right away to thank him, but she also wanted to give him time on Christmas morning to just be with his daughter. Christmas morning with young children was special. Helping him decorate his house for his six-year-old daughter had brought back wonderful memories of doing the same thing for Kristen.

She and Jake hadn't had much money when Kristen was little, but they'd filled their home with Christmas cheer just the same, mostly with lots of homemade decorations, like paper snowflakes hanging from the ceiling. Jeannie had even made a few stuffed toys for Kristen, although she'd never been the world's best seamstress. One of the toys had been a red-nosed reindeer. Kristen had loved that little reindeer. She'd lugged it around with her long after the season was over until the poor thing practically fell apart.

She'd told Raymond that story while they'd been out

shopping. The fact that he'd not only remembered but had found a way to give her a red-nosed reindeer of her own on Christmas morning made her love him all the more.

And she was in love. She could admit that to herself now. He wasn't Jake, but he shouldn't be Jake. She'd loved Jake with all her heart and she always would, but she wasn't looking to replace him. This was a brand new relationship, and the fact that she'd found love again astounded her.

They'd talked on the phone at least once a day since she'd flown back to Arizona. The minute her cell rang and the screen displayed his face (thanks to a silly picture she'd taken when they'd been in the year-round Christmas boutique), she felt a most wonderful kind of giddy excitement, almost like she was a teenager again.

Raymond was handling the lease for her new condo. The place would be ready for her the middle of January, but she'd decided not to move until the end of January. He'd offered to help her make the drive to Portland, a plan that met with Kristen's whole-hearted approval. Kristen said she was looking forward to meeting the man who'd swept her mother off her feet, although Jeannie got the feeling that Kristen would be looking at Raymond with a critical eye. He might even get the *you'd better be good to my mother* talk.

The prospect of moving into a place of her own was exciting and thrilling and overwhelming all at once. While it was true that Jeannie wouldn't be moving back to her old hometown, she didn't need to. Just like she wasn't trying to replace Jake with a new man, she wasn't trying to recreate her old life either. She was starting a new one, and that was the way it should be.

Apparently she wasn't the only one who thought Jeannie was ready to shake up her life.

A package had arrived the day before postmarked from New York City. Inside were an upscale set of watercolors, a variety of brushes, and three pads of watercolor paper. A note accompanying the gift simply said *Get busy, girlfriend. You've wasted enough time already! Marta.*

Maybe she had. She'd be rusty, but Marta had given her more than enough paper to practice on. And wasn't all art practice anyway? Her old high school art teacher had stressed that no piece of art was ever truly done, and everything an artist did was practice for the next piece. *As long as you try,* she'd said, *you'll pass my class with flying colors.*

That had been one disappointing thing about the reunion. None of Jeannie's old teachers had been there. But after she got moved into her condo, she might be able to look up the teachers who'd been important to her, if for nothing else than to let them know she was grateful for all they'd done for her. Especially her art teacher.

Jeannie hadn't expected to receive a present from Marta, and she'd told her that when she called to thank Marta for the paints.

"Invite me to your wedding and we'll call it even," Marta had said.

Jeannie had sputtered, her cheeks on fire, while Marta had laughed good-naturedly.

"I saw that kiss on the dance floor, girlfriend," she'd said. "You're smitten. Admit it."

Jeannie had—there was no reason to deny it—and they'd spent the next half hour talking about all sorts of things. Marta was spending Christmas with her artsy-fartsy friends, she'd said, and she sounded happy. She'd sold another painting while she was at the reunion, and there was the possibility of additional sales to the same collector.

"Who knows," she'd said. "I might become the next 'thing' in the art world."

Jeannie reminded her that she already was a "thing" in the art world, just like she'd been a "thing" in high school. "People remember you," she'd said.

"They remember you too," Marta had said. "You just never believed it until now."

Jeannie's talk with Cissy had gone a long way to convince her of that.

They'd ended the call with a promise to talk again before the New Year. Jeannie intended to keep that promise.

She sat contemplating the flowers with an artist's eye. Maybe she'd start off by practicing on these flowers. She could almost envision the painting—something with a pastel wash in the background and dreamy red blooms. The kind of computer graphic work Jeannie did at work always had well-defined edges, easy-to-read designs.

Watercolors produced softer images. Gentle blends of color. Images seen through the haze of loving memories.

At least, that was Jeannie's version of watercolor paintings. Her art teacher had looked at the few watercolors Jeannie had painted and told her she thought Jeannie had an old soul.

An old soul? Maybe. A happy soul and a full heart? Definitely.

Her cell vibrated against her leg. When she took her cell out of pocket, Raymond's face filled the display. Not only had she taken his picture at the boutique that day, he'd taken hers as well for his phone. She'd made a silly face right when Raymond snapped the picture. She couldn't help it. He hadn't made a silly face though. He'd just smiled that incredibly handsome smile of his when she'd taken his picture, and that's what greeted her now.

That warm, excited feeling spread through her again, and she smiled without even thinking about it. He just made her that happy.

"Merry Christmas," she said instead of hello. "Thank you for the wonderful flowers."

She heard the happy sounds of a six-year-old pounding on a toy keyboard in the background. Raymond had told Jeannie that he'd bought his daughter —Marri, short for Marrissa—a roll-up electronic keyboard for Christmas. Apparently it was a hit.

The thought of having a young child in her life again was a little daunting. Kristen had been an adult long enough that Jeannie had forgotten a lot of what she'd known about children Marri's age, but she figured it would come back to her.

"And thank you for your gift," he said. "It was driving me crazy, not opening it until Christmas morning. I think I was as excited as Marri was for all her Santa presents."

"You like it?"

Jeannie had been a little apprehensive about the gift. What do you get a man you've just started to date? She hadn't had much time to shop, but she'd found something she thought would work—a small digital recorder. *So we can make our own musical memories,* she'd written on the note that accompanied the recorder.

"I love it," he said.

She'd tried to find a cassette recorder and a few blank cassette tapes, but she might as well have been looking for eight-track tapes in the few stores she'd had time to go to while he'd been at his office.

She hadn't signed the note *Love, Jeannie,* just like he hadn't signed the card that came with the flowers *Love, Raymond.* But the feelings were there, plain as day, in everything they said and did for each other. They'd say the words when the time was right.

"I should let you get back to your family," he said. "You probably have a busy day planned."

"I'm actually giving them some space," she said. "It's their first Christmas together."

"So that means we can talk for a while?"

She settled back in her chair and tucked her legs beneath her. "As long as your daughter lets you," she said.

He chuckled. "My budding musical genius. My ex is going to kill me."

"You could have given her an electronic drum set," Jeannie said. "Or a tambourine."

Or a pony. He'd confessed that he'd almost set up his ex's new husband to buy Marri a pony for Christmas, but he'd stopped himself just in time.

"I'm not that cruel," he said.

No, he wasn't. He was a loving, kind-hearted man. Handsome and caring and someone she could see herself spending the rest of her life with. Whenever she was with him, even just talking on the phone, she felt like she'd found the best present ever under her Christmas tree.

And the best part of it all was that they were just at the beginning of what she knew would be a wonderful life together full of love and laughter.

Jeannie couldn't wait to get started.

Wedding chapel owner Edwina Morrisey loves her job, but after years of standing at the altar with someone else's Mr. Right, she wants to find a Mr. Right of her own. She wants romance. She wants love. And she'd really like a little nooky before she's too old to enjoy it. Hard to find in the tiny Nevada town of Liberty Springs.

Thomas Trask has grown disillusioned with performing weddings. He still believes in the concept of true love, he just doesn't see it often in the couples he marries at his chapel in Lovelock, Nevada. And he's never found true love for himself.

Or so he thought until his online friend Edwina places her picture and an ad on her chapel's website advertising for romance—age not a factor.

The ad will change both of their lives forever.

Edwina's overwhelmed (and Liberty Springs is overrun) by dozens of geriatric Lotharios—and one very handsome movie star lookalike—all intent on courting her. As for Thomas, he can't stop thinking about his beautiful friend Edwina, which makes him realize he's been in love with her for years. Could she possibly have feelings for him too? Only one way to find out: travel to Liberty Springs to meet her in person and hope they can find their own happily ever after.

WEDDING BELLE BLUES *is available from your favorite ebook distributor!*

ABOUT THE AUTHOR

A prolific, versatile, and award-winning writer, Annie Reed's written more short fiction than she can count. She's a frequent contributor to *Pulphouse Fiction Magazine* and *Mystery, Crime and Mayhem*. Her stories have appeared in numerous annual year's best mystery volumes. She's even had a story selected for inclusion in study materials for Japanese college entrance exams. Her *Unexpected* series of short-story collections showcase some of the best of her work.

Her longer works include *Gray Lady Rising* and *Gray Lady's Revenge*, co-authored with best-selling writer Robert Jeschonek, crime novels *Road of No Return, Pretty Little Horses, Paper Bullets*, and *A Death in Cumberland*, and novellas *The Wizard Behind the Curtain, Unbroken Familiar*, and *In Dreams*.

Annie writes mystery, science fiction, and fantasy under her own name and suspense as Kris Sparks. She also writes the Liberty Springs sweet romance novels under the name Liz McKnight. She can be found on the web at https://anniereed.wordpress.com/.

~

A Special Request from the author:

Word of mouth is critical for any author to succeed. If you enjoyed this book, please consider leaving a review at the site where you purchased it. Even a line or two would make all the difference in the world and I would greatly appreciate it.

Thank you!

ALSO BY ANNIE REED

ABBY MAXON MYSTERIES

Pretty Little Horses

Paper Bullets

MORETOWN BAY SERIES

Unbroken Familiar

Iris & Ivy

Tales from the Shadows

Not What They Seem

Spells Gone Bad

The Diz & Dee Holiday Mysteries

STANDALONE NOVELS

In Dreams

A Death in Cumberland

Faster

Road of No Return

Gray Lady Rising (co-authored with Robert Jeschonek)

Gray Lady's Revenge (co-authored with Robert Jeschonek)

UNEXPECTED SERIES

Unexpected Aliens

Unexpected Monsters

Unexpected Holidays

Unexpected Criminals

Unexpected Good Guys

Unexpected Futures

Unexpected Encounters

Unexpected Travels

Unexpected Hauntings

Unexpected Family

Unexpected Critters

Unexpected Killers

Unexpected Christmas

Unexpected Cats

COLLECTIONS

Crimes of Yesteryear

Everyday Magic

Life with Cats

Magic of the Heart

Turning the Page

Eight from the Silver State

The Patient Z Files